By the same author:

 **Belfast Girls**

 **Danger Danger**

 **Angel in Flight:**
an Angel Murphy thriller

Cover design: Raymond McCullough
(cover painting by **Ken Riddles**)

The Seanachie:
Tales of Old Seamus

Gerry McCullough

Reviews of **Belfast Girls**:

"fascinating ... original ... multilayered ... expertly travels from one genre to the next"
Kellie Chambers, **Ulster Tatler** (Book of the Month)

"romance at the core ... enriched with breathtaking action, mystery, suspense and some tear-jerking moments of tragedy.
Sheila M. Belshaw, author

"What starts out as a crime thriller quickly evolves into a literary festival beyond the boundary of genres"
PD Allen, author

Reviews of **Danger Danger**:

"starts with a bang and never quite lets up on the tension ... it will hook you from the beginning and keep you spell bound until the very last sentence."
Ellen Fritz, **Books 4 Tomorrow**

"The emotional intensity of the characters is beautifully drawn ... You care for these people."
Stacey Danson, author

an amazing, page turning, stunning novel ... equal to Belfast Girls in every respect. I can't wait for her next novel to be published.
Teresa Geering, author

an attention-grabbing plot, strong writing, and vivid characterization, ... fast-paced and highly addictive
L. Anne Carrington, author

The Seanachie:
Tales of Old Seamus

Gerry McCullough

Published by

www.preciousoil.com/publications

Copyright © **Gerry McCullough**, 2012

The right of **Gerry McCullough** to be identified as author of this work has been asserted by her in accordance with the **Copyright, Design and Patents Act, 1988**

ISBN 13: 978-0 9525785 5 0
ISBN 10: 0 9525785 5 7

First published **2012**

All rights reserved.

No part of this publication may be reproduced or transmitted in any form or by any means, electronic or mechanical, including photocopy, recording, or any information storage and retrieval system, without permission in writing from the publisher.

All characters are fictional, and any resemblance to anyone living or dead is accidental.

10a Listooder Road, Crossgar,
Downpatrick, Northern Ireland BT30 9JE

Contents

1	The Tale of a Teacup	1
2	The Horse Who Wouldn't Gallop	7
3	Annie's Apple Tree	13
4	McCafferty's Prize Pig	19
5	The Parish Outing	27
6	The Singing Dog	33
7	The Cuckoo Clock	41
8	The Mill Pool	49
9	At the Summer Fair	55
10	Miracle at Ardnakil	63
11	Two Different Valentines	71
12	Miss O'Sullivan's Secret	79
	About the author	87

Thanks to my husband, Raymond, for cover design, proof-reading the manuscript, editing and general encouragement.

1 The Tale of a Teacup

Whenever I can, I like to spend a week, or even a long weekend, in Ardnakil, the small Donegal village where I used to come to visit my grandparents many – too many – years ago. And when I'm there, I take the opportunity to call in on old Seamus O'Hare.

Seamus taught me everything I know about fishing, poaching, and the countryside. He taught me to recognise a lark's call, and to tell a wagtail from a chaffinch. He was a never ending source of stories about the people of the village and the townland, although I have reason to believe he kept most of his information back from my young ears. Now that I am no longer an innocent child, he is more forthcoming.

I can usually find Seamus at the bar of the local pub, *The Golden Pheasant*, sitting peacefully with a pint in one hand and his disreputable old pipe in the other, and always ready for what he calls, 'a bit of a crack.' He greets me with a smile and an invitation to join him, and before many minutes have passed he will be fairly launched into one of his stories. I listen with all the delight of my childhood days, but with rather more understanding of my fellow beings to add to the enjoyment.

It was one stormy evening late last November that Seamus told me the story of Maggie Neeson and the cracked teacup.

"Maggie lived in the last cottage out towards Millerstown, just where the houses start to straggle out and come to an end," said Seamus, puffing gently on his old pipe. "She was a quiet sort of a girl, and everyone was surprised when big Peter Malone started courting her, and after a reasonable space of time – it would have been about five years – got to the stage of proposing. Maggie took him. I suppose she liked him all right, but there was this as well, fellas don't grow on trees, and Maggie wasn't getting any younger. Sure, she had to take her chance when she could, and Peter wasn't a bad sort of a critter, though a bit tight with the money.

The Seanachie: Tales of Old Seamus – *Gerry McCullough*

Well, that was the start of the trouble. While he was still courting Maggie, Peter knew he had to spend a bit. Nothing too extravagant, you understand. A bar of chocolate once a month, and sometimes a few flowers that he could pick for free along the side of the road. He even took her into Millerstown a couple of times to the pictures, and for a cup of tea after.

But once she'd said yes, I reckon Peter felt he didn't need to bother any more. As he said to Maggie, 'Sure, we'll need every penny to pay for the week in Bundoran for the honeymoon. Where would I be getting the spare cash for gallivanting, or for buying presents, these days?'

Maggie didn't like it. She had her heart set on a fancy tea set she'd seen in the big china shop in Millerstown, and she was for buying it as a wedding present to herself, as she put it.

'We'll have all the neighbours calling in to see us, and expecting a cup of tea in a nice china set, Peter,' she told him. 'It's not very dear, considering.'

But Peter went on saying no, until the day Maggie went into Millerstown herself on the bus, and bought the set and carried it home with her.

Now, it was her own money Maggie used. She kept hens, and had a brave good turnover from the eggs, as well as selling the extra fowls to Liam McKenna the butcher, so she felt she had a right to spend her own money if she wanted to.

But Peter didn't see it like that. As far as he was concerned, Maggie was promised to him, and her money would be his money before long. So he didn't want her spending it instead of keeping it for him.

I just happened to be lying out in the long grass on the bank of the stream behind Maggie's cottage, watching for a chance to tickle an old trout that I'd had my eye on for days, and I couldn't help but hear the shouts of Peter when Maggie showed him the teaset.

'Wasting good money!' he was roaring. 'Take it back, woman, and get your money back while you still can! That's my last word on the subject!'

'I will not!' Maggie shouted back at him. 'I've wanted a good china set all my life, and if I can't buy one when I'm getting married, sure, when can I ever? You're an old skinflint, Peter Malone, and it's not even your money!'

1 The Tale of a Teacup

Peter let out a roar, and he must have grabbed one of the cups out of Maggie's hand, for she called out, 'Peter! Be careful, will you?'

'Ah, sure, why should I be careful with it?' Peter roared. 'It's not my money that bought it, you tell me!'

And with that, he must have hurled the cup across the room, for Maggie let out a wail to Peter to let the cup alone, and I heard her rushing across the room after it.

By then things had got a bit confused.

Now, so far I haven't mentioned young Chuck Doherty, as he called himself.

Chuck was a son of my old friend Sean Doherty, who emigrated to the USA when he was only a lad. Young Chuck had come back to the village on a sort of holiday – a vacation, he called it – just about the time that Peter and Maggie had got engaged.

I don't know if you've ever noticed it, but it's a thing I've often thought about, that when something seems valuable to one person, it starts a good many other people off thinking the same.

Before Peter started courting Maggie, no one else ever took a bit of notice of her. But no sooner did the fellas round about see that Peter wanted her, than a number of them began to think that there might be more to Maggie than they realised.

And of all of them, it was young Chuck Doherty that thought the most of her.

Just the evening before Maggie bought the tea set, Chuck was in this very bar, sitting with me, and after the first pint or so, he began to talk more confidentially, as people do.

'I love that girl, Seamus,' he said to me, very earnest. 'I used to dream, when I was home in the States, of a beautiful young Irish colleen, and when I came back here, the first girl I saw was Maggie, and she was just my dream come true. What she sees in that big lout Malone, I'll never know. I just wish I had a chance to show her how much I love her.' He laughed, in a shame faced sort of way. 'I used to dream, when I thought of my Irish colleen, that I would win her heart by rescuing her from a dragon or something. If I could just rescue her from that Peter Malone guy, I guess that would be enough!'

'Well, you never know, Chuck lad,' I told him. 'Stick around, and maybe you'll get a chance to do just that.'

The Seanachie: Tales of Old Seamus – *Gerry McCullough*

Lying in the grass behind Maggie's cottage, it came to me that maybe this was Chuck's chance.

I got myself away from there without them hearing a thing, though by then the row was bad enough that they might not have heard if the house had fallen down.

Chuck was mooning around throwing bits of stick into the lake. It only took me a couple of minutes to find him.

'If you want to rescue an Irish colleen,' I told him, 'now's your chance.'

I'll say this for him, he didn't need telling twice. He was away up the road to the cottage in no time at all.

I followed him a bit more slowly. I didn't want to miss anything, you understand, but I didn't fancy getting into a fight either. At my time of life, you leave all that to the young ones.

I got to the cottage door just in time to see what happened.

Peter Malone, with his arms up protecting his head, was running down the path for dear life, letting out roar after roar. 'Ah, don't now, Maggie! Don't now, Maggie!'

After him came Maggie, the big broom in her hands, and she was beating Peter round the lugs with it as hard as she could go. She got two or three good blows in while I was watching, and I reckon they weren't the first.

'Break my good china cup, would you?' she was shouting at him. 'A crack a mile long, there is in it, Peter Malone! Just you wait till I get at you!'

But Peter, showing more sense than I would have credited him with, had no notion of waiting. With a roar, he was off down the road, leaving Maggie, flushed and victorious, waving the broom after him.

As she turned round to set the broom down, she saw Chuck, standing there with his mouth open.

'Well, what are you looking at?' she snapped. 'Are you coming in, or aren't you?'

Chuck followed her meekly into the cottage.

How they worked it out between them I can't tell you, for they closed the door tight. All I can tell you is that they weren't shouting.

I still get a postcard from them both occasionally, from the States, for she married him and moved out there within a very short time.

1 The Tale of a Teacup

But whether Chuck thinks he ended up with the Irish colleen or with the dragon, I've never dared to ask.

2 The Horse Who Wouldn't Gallop

It was spring, and I had taken myself up to spend a long weekend in Ardnakil, the small Donegal village where I own a small, whitewashed cottage, left to me by my grandparents. And as always when I'm there, I wanted to hook up with my friend old Seamus O'Hare.

As often, I found Seamus at the bar of the local pub, *The Golden Pheasant*, sitting peacefully with a pint in one hand and his disreputable old pipe in the other, and always ready for what he calls 'a bit of a crack.' It was a fine late spring evening, and the bar was full of comment about the results of the Grand National that afternoon.

'I'm not a betting man myself,' Seamus said to me as I joined him and commented on the race. 'But I've always liked horses. Like my friend Barney O'Callaghan. Did I ever tell you the story of Barney O'Callaghan and the horse who wouldn't gallop?'

'No, Seamus,' I said. 'Tell me now.' And without more ado, he did.

'Barney,' he began, 'was what they call a character. A rogue, you might say, a fella who'd sell his granny for sixpence, but for all that the type of critter who you couldn't help liking. He had a great way with the women. One and all they fell for him, though you would think they would have the sense to know better. It was never long before they found out what he was really like. He'd swear black was white, looking at you as bold as brass, but with a twinkle in his eye that made you think he was as honest as a Saint.

I've seen him stand and chat with the well-off Dublin men who used to rent the big houses for the shooting, and sympathise with them for the scarcity of pheasants that year, and him with his back pockets crammed full of the birds!

Barney was a great man with the horses. He never held down a regular job with any stable that I heard tell of, but he could always get a few days or weeks work when he wanted to. The owners knew any horse would eat out of his hand, and there was no one like him

The Seanachie: Tales of Old Seamus – *Gerry McCullough*

when it came to getting a lazy or an out of condition animal ready for a race.

I believe if he'd wanted to he could have had a good job in Kildare at some of the big stables. But no, Barney preferred to mooch around here, doing odd jobs when he needed to and mostly making an easy living. And who should blame him? – Except when it came to the poaching, or maybe worse.

I knew more about Barney than most did, for I like to spend my time lying by the streams on a summer's day, or dandering through the meadows. Many's the time I used to see him up to his tricks, when I was resting on my back half hidden in the long summer grass, gazing at the clear sky and following the flight of a lark.

One fine night – it was a good many years ago now – I had gone out late to see if I could see a badger, when I heard a noise of something coming – oh, very careful and stealthy – through the woods. It was too loud to be a man, and yet it was no wild animal that I had ever come across, for it was too quiet and controlled.

I was curious, I don't mind admitting. I slipped silently behind the nearest large tree, and watched. In a few moments I saw what was making the noise. It was a man, going very slowly and with hardly a sound, and leading a horse. The horse was making very little noise either. I guessed that its bridle and hoofs were muffled with cloths.

I'm a man with my share of curiosity, I don't mind owning, and I would say I can move quieter than most. At any rate, I slipped through the woods like any shadow, and neither the man nor his horse seemed to sense that I was there.

It wasn't possible to tell who the man might be for a while, for it was dark enough in the wood, with only the odd shaft of moonlight, but after a bit I heard him whispering and I caught the words, 'Whoa, old fella,' and then, 'Soon be home now, my honey,' and I had a sort of half guess that it was Barney, for I'd heard him talking like that to horses before. And after another while it happened that the moon caught his face and lit it up plain enough to see.

Now, whatever Barney O'Callaghan was doing in the woods with a horse which didn't belong to him, I was pretty sure it was no good, so I kept on following him until we all three came out at the edge of the wood. I had to drop back a bit as Barney led the horse across a field

2 The Horse Who Wouldn't Gallop

or two, but he was keeping close to the hedges himself, and that made it easier.

I was still behind him when we came out at a big house which I recognised as Milray Lodge, Mr Brendan McGarvey's place. McGarvey was a big, burly, red-faced man, and he kept two or three horses, which he would race occasionally when the notion took him, so it was a good guess that this was one of his.

I could see that Barney was putting the horse away in its stable, and I thought it was time to slip away before he caught me. I thought a bit about what Barney was up to the next day or two, and made a few inquiries from some of the racing men in the locality. I didn't think it was up to me to run telling tales of Barney to Mr Brendan McGarvey, a man I never liked much. But I had a shrewd suspicion the whole business was connected in some way with horse racing.

When I heard from one or two different sources that *Summer Lightning*, McGarvey's newest horse, was proving a big disappointment to its owner, I thought I was on to the truth. *Summer Lightning*, old Peter Kilrush told me, was McGarvey's pride and joy, and he had been looking to win with him in all the local races at least, and maybe take him across the water if all went well. But in his last few trials, it seemed, the animal had hardly been able to do more than canter, and never got as far as a good gallop at all.

McGarvey thought *Summer Lightning* might be sickening for something, but he didn't want to give up on him yet. He was determined to try him out in one or two races at least. It seemed to me only too likely that Barney was doping the horse some way or other to bring down its speed. That would mean that the odds against *Summer Lightning* would go up, and a betting man like Barney could make himself an easy bit of money, if the horse was let alone to run at its real speed on the day of the race.

The next night, I hung about near Barney's cottage, taking care to keep out of sight. It was dusk when he came out, a lovely mild evening when the world seemed full of peace and tranquillity. I dandered along the lanes and hedgerows after Barney, sniffing the scent of the bluebells and the wild garlic, and wasn't too surprised when we finished up at Milray Lodge.

I hung back until Barney came out, quiet as a cat after a song-thrush, with *Summer Lightning* following softly behind. It was a wonder to me that Barney was able to persuade the horse to come without making the sort of noise someone would notice, but there, as I said, Barney had a great way with horses. I followed the pair of them back through the woods where I'd seen them first, and it was then that it began to get interesting.

I mentioned, didn't I, that Barney had a great way not only with the horses, but with the women? Well, about a dozen years before the events of this story, he'd courted and married one of them – a fine, upstanding lass of the name of Katie Reilly. It didn't last, of course. Whether she threw him out or he left her I couldn't say, but there it was – they went their separate ways.

Katie was left with a young daughter and she made a living serving in Halloran's pub. It came to me with a shock of surprise that Barney was making for the wee cottage where Katie and the child lived. I watched as Barney tied *Summer Lightning* to a tree and went nearer to the cottage. He whistled once or twice, and then came an answering whistle.

I thought to myself that Katie Reilly had changed if she was fool enough to get mixed up with Barney O'Callaghan again after what she'd been through, and that it wasn't like Katie to be whistling to him. Then someone slipped cautiously out of the cottage, and I saw that it wasn't Katie.

The wean had grown, of course, since I'd last seen or thought of her. Nine or ten, she must be. And there was something wrong with her leg, for she had a crutch to help her along, but she was managing fine with it. I remembered something I'd heard a while back about Katie's daughter being ill – polio, was it? – but I couldn't remember the details.

'Oh, Da! You managed to bring him again!' the lass was saying.

'I can't do it much more,' said Barney. 'They'll find out for sure sooner or later. But I thought I'd come this time anyway, seeing it's your birthday. Don't say your Daddy never gave you anything!'

'Oh, Da! I do love you so! This is my best birthday present ever!'

'Come on, now, Aine,' Barney said, 'come and I'll help you up. And for pity's sake don't be galloping the poor beast so hard this time! Leave him some puff for when auld McGarvey wants to have a go on him!'

2 The Horse Who Wouldn't Gallop

Aine laughed. She threw her arms round her father's neck, and hugged him until it looked as if she'd burst. I caught a glimpse of her face, glowing with joy, as she hugged *Summer Lightning*'s neck in turn and showered kisses on his soft nose. Barney threw her up on the horse, and then she was off, heading for the bridle paths over the open ground behind the cottage. It was dusk and growing darker, but there should be enough light for a skilful rider for another hour or so yet.

Barney stood gazing after her. There was a look on his face that I never saw there before. Then he threw himself down on the grass and waited for Aine to come back. I supposed that when she did, Barney would wait until it was fully dark before returning the borrowed horse to its rightful owner.

I had to admit to myself that I had guessed wrong about the whole business. For once in his life, Barney O'Callagan's actions were motivated by someone other than himself. Certainly, he had no business to borrow Mr Brendan McGarvey's horse so that his lame daughter should be able to enjoy something that meant so much to her.

In a way, you might say it was typical of Barney to do a good deed in a crooked way. But one thing I was sure about. I had no right to hang about watching Barney or Aine any longer. It was simply not my business.

After a while, I melted quietly back into the woods, and through the stillness of the gentle summer night I made my way homewards.

3 Annie's Apple Tree

The hot sun beat down on my shoulders. High in the blue, blue sky above me, a lark circled and sang. I stretched back lazily on the river bank, lit my pipe, and watched my old friend Seamus O'Hare as he expertly cast his line over the chuckling brown waters of the little stream.

I had known Seamus for many years, since, as a child, growing up in the small village of Ardnakil, in Donegal, I had learned country lore from him over the happy summer days, everything from how to recognise a lark's call, to how to tickle trout in the deep, quiet reaches of the mountain burns.

As I watched him, it occurred to me to wonder why Seamus was openly fishing this river, instead of, as had been his wont, going stealthily to a remote area, where he could poach the waters in safety, and I asked that question, with the freedom of an old friend.

'Why,' replied Seamus, 'myself and the owner of this stream are on the best of terms, and I have a welcome to fish here whenever it suits me. Did I never tell you the story?'

'No, I don't believe you did, Seamus,' I answered him, leaning back more comfortably against a tussock of grass. In the distance the song of a blackbird echoed round us. The only other sound was the faint ringing of sheep bells. The sun shone from a soft blue stretch of sky. 'Why don't you tell me it now?'

'Well, now,' began Seamus, 'you see the little cottage just over the next ridge?'

I sat up a little to peer after his pointing finger, and could just discern a small, neat looking cottage fresh with whitewash, with a comfortable haze of soft smoke floating lazily from its chimney. I could see little of its garden at that distance, but flashes of colour suggested flowers in plenty, and to one side of the low roof there was

The Seanachie: Tales of Old Seamus – *Gerry McCullough*

a tree with wide spreading branches, whose pink blossoms promised a rich harvest of apples in the autumn.

'That cottage is the home of an old friend of mine, Annie O'Grady,' Seamus said. 'I've known Annie, and her man Sean, since I was a lad the size of sixpence, mitching off from school on bright spring days and giving Sean a hand with the tatie planting. Sean and me were pals, good pals, although he was three times my age, and Annie was a second mother to me. Many's the time I sat at their table and ate Annie's apple tart, fresh home-made from the apples on her tree. No apples like those, Annie always said. Sean planted the tree from a shoot when they were first wed, and it had grown along with their marriage. And because there were no childer of the marriage, I guess Annie had a special affection for the tree, almost as if it took the place of a child.

There came the time when Sean grew old and died. I won't conceal from you that I wept for him. It was a sore loss for me. Annie looked older suddenly, and I made sure I called with her as often as ever, or more, and I thought to myself that she clung to the apple tree in a new way. It seemed to mean something to her, beyond understanding.

It was some time after that, though many years ago now, that I called at Annie's cottage one bright summer afternoon, and found her weeping by the empty fireplace.

'Why, Annie!' I said. 'Whatever ails you?'

At first she was for drying her tears and pretending to smile, as if it were nothing, but I wouldn't have it, and before long I had dragged the story out of her.

The cottage, I knew, was rented, and the owner was the Hon. Marjorie Fitzpatrick, a rich woman mostly living in Dublin, though times she would stay in the big house in the estate across the fields from Annie's cottage. This Hon. Marjorie was a sharp spoken woman with what I would call an English accent, though I'm told it's only Dublin. A tall, commandeering woman, good-looking in her way, but not a cuddlesome sort that a man would want for his wife.

Well, it seemed this woman Fitzpatrick had written to Annie to say that the lease for the cottage was nearly up, and that she would be obliged if Annie would make plans to vacate the cottage when the time was due. She was giving Annie six months, which she felt was ample notice, and remained hers faithfully, M. H. Fitzpatrick. P.S.

3 Annie's Apple Tree

She felt she should explain that there was nothing personal against Annie, who had been a good tenant, but she had had a very good offer for the cottage and intended to sell it. Annie probably knew that the demand for cottages in Donegal was increasing at a great rate, and as a business woman, this was an offer she could not refuse. M.H.F.

'I knew it was only a lease,' Annie wept, 'but I never thought she wouldn't renew it. Sean and me started our married life here, and I can't bear to go elsewhere. I could move in with our Maureen, my sister, in Donegal Town, but what would I do with Sean's apple tree? I couldn't dig it up, and if I did Maureen has no garden to plant it in!'

And she wept as if her heart would break. It was the apple tree, I could see, that was the heart of her sorrow.

Now, I'll not deny that I was angry. It seemed to me a selfish act, by this Hon Marjorie Fitzpatrick, to drive an old woman from the house she had lived in for so long, just for the sake of the money she would make by it. I went home and sat by my own fireplace that evening, and I thought long and hard, and I wondered what there was that I could do to help Annie. It seemed to me that in the six months left to her, I would be a fool if I couldn't think of something.

A few days later, it began to look as if things were working out for me. It was rumoured all over the neighbourhood that the Hon. Marjorie was coming down for one of her visits to *Carmarnock House*, the home of her ancestors for many a year. I had no relationship or friendship with the Hon. Marjorie, but I wondered if maybe I could bring one about, get on speaking terms with the lady, and put in a good word for poor Annie.

However, the first I saw of her was in the village street, when I was just coming out of *The Golden Pheasant* after doing a bit of business with the landlord. She was standing in the centre of the road, her legs planted astride, her hands plunged in the pockets of her tweed jacket, and her head flung back in a burst of laughter that echoed from here to the Errigal mountain.

'It's Seamus O'Hare, isn't it?' she demanded, coming over to me. 'I recognise you, my man. I know all about you and your poaching! Well, let me take this opportunity of warning you that if I catch you poaching fish from my stream, and selling it to your friend Willie Brennan there in *The Golden Pheasant*, as I know well you do, it'll be the worse for you!'

The Seanachie: Tales of Old Seamus – *Gerry McCullough*

'Indeed, I never have and never will do such a thing, m'am!' I protested, and I spoke the simple truth. I never sold fish from her stream to *The Golden Pheasant,* for the landlord there wanted only salmon, which I was able to get from Lord Kilnevin's loch. I always had to go much further afield to get rid of the Hon. Marjorie's trout.

But whether or not she believed me, it didn't seem like a hopeful start to a plea for Annie.

It was about a week after this that the news began to go round. There had been a break-in at Carnmarnock House. A lot of jewellery had been stolen, and a silver medal, first prize in the Galway Races, which the Hon Marjorie's father had won when he was just a young lad. It seemed that she was more concerned about the medal than any of the rest, although some of the jewellery was valuable enough.

I kept my ears open, and picked up what information I could.

That evening, I went boldly up to the front entrance to Carmarnock House, my hat in my hand, and asked to speak to the Hon. Marjorie.

The manservant who opened the door didn't seem very happy to see me. He said, 'Wait there,' and shut the door in my face.

However, in a few minutes he came back, and told me to follow him.

The Hon. Marjorie was standing in front of the large fireplace, poking restlessly at the smouldering turf fire with one foot, which was clad in a heavy brogue shoe.

'Well?' she snapped. 'What do you want here, Seamus O'Hare?'

'I heard something today which I thought might help you, ma'm,' I said. 'It's about your jewels and the medal that were stolen.'

At that she looked up sharply and began to take much more of an interest.

'What, do you think you know who stole them?' she asked eagerly.

'It's a possibility, ma'm. I can't say more than that.' I paused for a moment, then I went on slowly. 'I don't want to get anyone into trouble, but I overheard something earlier today, and it makes me fairly confident that the things were taken by a young fellow of the name of Brian McKenna. He'll have hidden them away somewhere, and I don't have any idea where. But what I was thinking – 'I paused again.

'Well?' asked the Hon Marjorie impatiently.

'He's not such a bad youngster, ma'm. I thought, if it was put to him the right way, he might be persuaded to return the stuff. Especially

3 Annie's Apple Tree

if you were ready to let the matter drop if you got your things back safely.'

'Hmm,' said the Hon Marjorie. She thought for a minute. 'Who is this Brian McKenna? I don't seem to recognise his name. Where would we find him?'

'He's not local. I wouldn't know where to find him, myself. That's the problem.'

The Hon. Marjorie thought some more. Eventually she looked up. 'Seamus,' she said, 'as long as I get my father's medal back, I don't care about anything else. I'd like the jewellery as well, mind. I wouldn't mind about letting the rascal off. But how are you going to get talking to the fellow if you don't know where he lives? And are you sure you can persuade him.?'

'Persuade him? Me?' I laughed. 'No, no, I don't know the youngster well enough to persuade him. But I know someone who does, and who would be bound to see him while he's in this part of the country. A lady who's been like a second mother to young Brian. He'll call in to see her for sure, and if she's willing to speak to him about it, she can show him the sense of taking up your offer. Mind you, she would have to be feeling pretty friendly towards yourself, before she would interfere.'

'And who would that be?' asked the Hon Marjorie a bit anxiously. Perhaps she realised that not everyone around the district was very well inclined towards her.

'Why, it's my old friend Annie O'Grady!' I said.

There was a silence for some minutes.

'Annie O'Grady?' said she slowly. 'Why, then, Seamus, there's no hope of her speaking up for me. She can't be feeling very kindly towards me just now, for I've refused to renew the lease of her cottage, and I know she wants me to.'

'Dear, dear,' I said, and I whistled, and made to seem very concerned. 'Well, ma'm,' I said, 'it's up to yourself, but if you want the jewels back –'

'– and the medal!' she interrupted.

'– yes, and the medal, then I think your only way is to write a letter to Annie O'Grady saying you've changed your mind and that you want to renew the lease after all. Better make it for a good long time, too. For as long as Annie's likely to be there. Then I'll take it round to her this afternoon, and talk to her about speaking to young Brian. I think I can get her to see it our way, as long as she knows you'll not be putting her out of the cottage.'

I never saw such a beaming face as the Hon. Marjorie had when she realised that she was probably going to get her jewels, and her father's medal, back! She sat down straight away, and wrote just what I suggested, and it was witnessed by myself and the manservant, just in case of accidents, as you might say.

I took it straight round to Annie, and explained to her what I'd arranged, and although she scolded me a bit at first, she was so delighted about the cottage that she agreed to go along with what I'd planned.

To cut a long story short, I was able to bring the jewels and the medal back to the Hon. Marjorie the following day, and she was so pleased that she straightaway gave me permission to fish in her stream any time I wanted! And her and me have been the best of friends ever since!'

'That was a lucky coincidence, wasn't it Seamus?' I said. 'The burglary, and Annie O'Grady knowing the thief so well?'

'Coincidence?' said Seamus. 'I wouldn't say this to anyone but yourself, but there was no coincidence! I planned the whole thing, burglary and all, on purpose, to save Annie's cottage. And no need for you to look shocked. Who was the worse off, tell me that? Annie got to keep her cottage and her precious apple tree. I made a friend, and got some good fishing rights, to say nothing of still enjoying Annie's apple pies!

The Hon. Marjorie got the opportunity to act kindly instead of selfishly, lost neither her jewels nor her father's medal, and made a good friend in myself into the bargain. And as for Brian McKenna, he suffered least of all, for there never was any such person! So you may take that look off your face, and come and have a go with this fishing rod, now, and see if you can catch as many trout as I can!'

4 McCafferty's Prize Pig

My old friend, Seamus O'Hare, sat at the bar in *The Golden Pheasant* and twinkled at me, his pipe in one hand and a pint of Guinness in the other.

'So you know nothing about livestock, you tell me?' he said. 'And you've been coming to Ardnakil for so many years? You shock me, Jamie.'

I smiled at him.

'You have to remember, I'm a city man, Seamus,' I said. 'All I know about country ways is what I've learnt from you. But I'm always willing to hear more.'

And in truth, whatever I knew about the ways of my forefathers and the country life, I had learnt from Seamus, since the days when I had visited Ardnakil as a child, and listened in fascination to his stories of the plants and birds and wildlife around me. No one knew more of country ways and days than my old friend Seamus O'Hare

'Well,' said Seamus, 'Maybe you'd like to hear a bit about my friend Brian McCafferty, who raised the best pigs in this region for over fifty years?'

'It depends, Seamus,' I said cautiously. 'Is it an interesting story, would you say? Pigs, now?'

'Interesting?' exclaimed Seamus. 'It depends what you call interesting!' And calling to Tommy the barman for another two pints, he sat back on his stool, pulled on his pipe, and began his story.

'It was a few years ago, now. Brian and me were friends from way back. We went to school together, and fought, at lunch time, with 'cheesers', as we called them then, from the chestnut trees they fell off. The English say conkers, I'm told. I was always the winner. Brian was very competitive, now. I won't say he didn't do well. But he didn't do as well as me, I have to say!

The Seanachie: Tales of Old Seamus – *Gerry McCullough*

Well, the times went past. We grew up. Brian had a farm of his own. His daddy's, of course. In those days, we expected to get enough from our fathers to keep us going. My own Da, good luck to him, never made enough to leave me anything – and, sure, why should he? I never made enough myself to matter.

Anyway, I think you could say that Brian still had the competitive spirit he had as a lad, with the chestnuts. Whatever he did, he wanted to win.

And what he was doing now was rearing pigs.

There was this competition.

The *'Donegal Prize Pig Award'*, it was called.

And Brian McCafferty had the winner, without a doubt, or so he said.

But then, there was Davy Maguire, from the other side of the valley, and according to Davy, the pig he had was bound to win over any other, McCafferty's not excepted.

The time came nearer to the competition, and the odds were growing shorter in the pubs, and no one would have wanted to hazard a guess as to which would be the winner – McCafferty's *'Pink Perfection'* or Maguire's *'Donegal Hero'*.

The rivalry caused a bit of bad feeling between McCafferty and Maguire, I'm sorry to say, and they would spend evening after evening in *The Golden Pheasant*, arguing and boasting. To tell you the truth, it made me laugh to see them, standing face to face, each with his jaw thrust out, and going at it hammer and tongs, for McCafferty was a thin slip of a man, while Maguire was a real giant – a big strong man with the arms of the village blacksmith in the song, *'Strong as iron bands'*. They made a right comic sight, squaring up to each other.

What's more, the rivalry carried on down to the next generation.

McCafferty was a married man, I'll have you know, and his eldest son, Mikey, a lad of eight or nine as I recall, was as eager as get out for his Da to win. While on the other hand his rival, Maguire, had a nephew of the same sort of age, who was equally keen to see his uncle Davy walk away with the prize.

So day by day, in the school playground, the pair of them were fighting the bit out, as to whether their da or their uncle would win the prize.

One fine day, not long before the judging was to take place at the Ardnakil Fair, matters came to a head.

4 McCafferty's Prize Pig

It was McCafferty's son, Mikey, who had the idea.

'Listen, now, Danny!' he exclaimed to Maguire's young nephew. 'I tell you how we can tell which pig is the better man! We'll get them both out of their sties one of these fine nights when no one's looking, and race them up O'Brien's Lane till we see which is the faster!'

It went down well, no doubt of it.

It was only Francis O'Sullivan, who knew far too much about everything, who pointed out to the lads that the prize for the best pig was nothing to do with speed.

'It's for the fattest pig, sure,' young Frankie said, 'so the one that can run fastest is likely to be the skinniest, not the fattest, do y' see?'

But nobody was listening to him, least of all young Mikey.

They laid their plans carefully. The race was to be for the next evening. Not too late, for it would be no race if it was too dark to see what the piggies were doing, but late enough so the evening feeds would be over, and the proud owners unlikely to come back until the morning. Around eight o'clock, they reckoned. It was June, and the sky would still be light enough for a few hours by then.

It just so happened that they discussed their plans behind the old mill down by O'Brien's Lane. No one was around, they thought. Aye, no one but myself, Seamus O'Hare, stretched out beside the hedge out of their sight, looking up at the sweet June sky, smelling the roses in the hedge, and enjoying the evening air. And listening, besides, to the plans the young rogues were making, and having a good chuckle to myself at the thought of the race they were planning.

Now, it wouldn't be Seamus O'Hare if I was to go running with tales. I couldn't for the life of me see what harm there might be in the youngsters' plans. Besides which, there was a bit of fun in it. And foreby, a bit of cash to be made on the side.

For young Frankie was right, no doubt of it. Whichever of the pigs had the fastest speed, would be the leanest, and so would be the loser in the fattest pig contest.

Down in *The Golden Pheasant*, they were running a book on the prize competition.

And I had a very good chance, if all went well with the piggy race, of knowing in advance which would win the big prize!

On the evening of the race, I positioned myself well, early on.

The Seanachie: Tales of Old Seamus – *Gerry McCullough*

It was a beautiful June evening, with the white blossoms of the hawthorn and the yellow whins and the pale wild roses scenting the air, and the sun lighting up the green meadows and the silky honey coloured coats of the cows who were still grazing as they waited for their farmers to take them in for the evening milking. The sheep and their young were nibbling contentedly at the short grass, and the lambs nudged against their mothers as they waited for the evening feed.

Presently there came the noise of young human voices, chattering excitedly as they surged up the lane, everyone of them wanting to get their say in over the rest.

'Why have you got young Timmy with you, Mikey?' I heard Danny Maguire exclaim. 'This is not for kids, sure! Timmy's only four, he should be in his bed.'

Mikey's voice sounded sulky.

'It's my Ma's fault, she said I had to look after him while she went out to the Bingo. I argued with her, but it was no use. I think she meant me to stay in with him and put him to bed, but, sure, he's happy enough to come out with us, and he won't be a nuisance, will you, Timmy?'

'No, Mikey,' responded the youngster happily.

'Well, let's get on with it,' said one of the other lads. 'I want to see these piggies run!'

So off went Mikey and Danny to the respective pig sties.

In a short enough time they were back, driving the two fat pigs before them. Fat, I say! It would have been a day's work to tell any difference between them, for they were both as round and soft and pink as a cloud at sunset, and to my eye neither of them looked like a champion runner!

There was a chatter and a fuss and a lot of excitement, and Mikey and Danny tried to bring their runners up to the starting point.

In fact, there was so much noise that it was no wonder that none of the lads noticed the other thing that was going on. Indeed, it was a few moments before I noticed it myself.

Now, I've already told you that I kept the boys' secret to myself, for fear of spoiling sport.

But with half the lads in the village in on the plot, it wasn't to be expected that no one else would get to hear of it.

And it seemed that that was what had happened.

4 McCafferty's Prize Pig

Young Pat Donnelly had talked to his best mate, Larry Cassidy behind the school bicycle shed, pouring out all the details in his great excitement, and unbeknown to him Big Jimmy Byrne had been listening. Jimmy told his mate Sean, Sean spread it around to the lads in *The Golden Pheasant* that night, and it wasn't long before it got to the ears of both McCafferty and Maguire.

At first they dismissed it as a load of rubbish, but come the time of the race, neither of them felt safe ignoring the tale. Separately – for they were by way of being sworn enemies by now – they talked it over with their friends and supporters, and decided that the only thing to do was to check up on *Pink Perfection* and *Donegal Hero*, to make sure the pigs were safely in their sties.

The bellow of rage McCafferty let out when he found the sty empty and no sign of *Pink Perfection,* was only equalled by the wails of grief that came from Maguire, when he realized that *Donegal Hero* was gone!

From my safe position behind the hedge, I heard a confused rumble of angry voices approaching up the lane.

Meanwhile, Mikey and Danny, both maneuvering their runners by the nose ring, and each with a big ash switch cut from the hedge to give the piggies the option to start, were nearly ready to begin the race.

The whole group of lads were gathered round the starting line, a chalk mark drawn across the dust of the lane. They were all so intent on the action that I felt I could risk pulling myself up for a quick glance over the hedge, to see better what was going on.

It was then that I noticed that there was no sign of young Timmy.

I stood up for a better look.

Yes, there he was, wandering off by himself down the middle of the lane, less interested in the race than in being out by himself so late at night, and eager to explore everything he could before big brother Mikey put a stop to it.

In another second he had disappeared from sight round a bend.

And it was at that exact second that Kevin Hardy, the starter, finished his 'One, two, three, Go!' and dropped his handkerchief.

Mikey and Danny released the pigs and gave them two almighty thwacks with their ash switches, and with loud yelps the piggies started off down the lane as if they had been fired from a cannon.

The Seanachie: Tales of Old Seamus – *Gerry McCullough*

Now you, Jamie, who tell me you know little of livestock, may not know that a charging pig in the prime of life is a dangerous animal.

In one more second I had leapt the hedge, and was shouting to the boys, 'Stop them! Young Timmy's right in their path! Stop them!'

Mikey and Danny stared at me thunderstruck.

The pigs were galloping on along the lane for dear life.

What could we do?

Then there was a noise like a whirlwind, and Davy Maguire was charging past us like greased lightening, both arms waving.

And as we watched, flabbergasted, he caught up with the pigs, seized the tail of each, and raised them by the hind feet off the ground.

How he had the strength to do it I'll never know.

However, he didn't have to hold them both for long, for a moment later, McCafferty was there, roaring down the lane behind him, and within seconds he had relieved Maguire of the weight of *Pink Perfection*, and before the awed spectators had properly taken in what was happening, both owners had managed to get control of the pigs by their nose rings.

There was a moment while everybody took a breath.

Then all hell broke loose.

I didn't stay for it.

As I slipped quietly away, I could hear McCafferty shouting at Mikey, and Maguire giving Danny an earful, and there was young Timmy wandering back round the corner smiling happily, as if nothing had happened and he'd been as safe as houses the whole time.

But when all was said and done, there was an outcome which took all Ardnakil by surprise, and that was that Brian McCafferty withdrew his prize pig, *Pink Perfection*, from the competition at the Ardnakil Fair for the *Donegal Prize Pig*.

There was great wonderment all around as to why he would have done this.

But I had it from McCafferty, in a quiet chat we had one night, that he couldn't bring himself to win over the man who had saved his young son Timmy, at least from serious injury if not indeed his life.

And from that day on McCafferty and Maguire were the best of friends.

I never repeated McCafferty's words to me to Davy Maguire.

4 McCafferty's Prize Pig

If he had heard McCafferty sounding so cock-sure of winning, it might have started the whole feud all over again.

5 The Parish Outing

It was a blazing hot summer's day in the small town of Ardnakil in Donegal, and I felt far too hot and lazy to do anything.

After all, I was on holiday, escaping from town life, and taking a well earned rest in the peaceful little cottage, set among the beautiful hills of Donegal, that I'd been visiting regularly since I lived there in my childhood.

I decided to take a short stroll in the shade of the leafy trees along the river bank, and there I found my old friend Seamus O'Hare, taking his ease in a patch of shadow beneath a full leaved chestnut tree.

I threw myself down beside him and stretched out luxuriously, and for a few minutes neither of us spoke.

The sound of the river bubbling along contentedly beside us was refreshment to the spirit.

Not far off, a bright kingfisher hung poised above the cool waters, ready to dive on its prey. A flash of blue told me he had plunged down.

'What a day,' said Seamus at last. 'We don't get many of them. Just the day that would be perfect for the parish outing next week. But there, it may well be pouring by then!' He chuckled mischievously.

'Parish outing?' I inquired lazily. 'What would that be, Seamus?'

'Don't tell me you've never been on a parish outing, Jamie?' asked Seamus in surprise. 'And you that's been coming to Ardnakil since you were the size of sixpence? Well, well!'

'I must have missed them all,' I said. 'Tell me more.'

'Many a thing happens on those parish outings,' said Seamus, smiling reminiscently. 'I could tell you some stories!'

'Go on, then,' I said.

It was enough.

'Well, now,' said Seamus, leaning back on the soft, fresh, green bank and chewing at a piece of grass as he spoke. 'What can I tell you? I remember the time,' he said, 'when there was hardly a soul in the

The Seanachie: Tales of Old Seamus – *Gerry McCullough*

town didn't go on the outings. It didn't matter what the outing was for, the parish school or the choir or even the Women's Meeting, the whole clatter of us went, and not just the children, like now. It was a good opportunity for a fella to get a bit more friendly with a girl he might have had his eye on for a while.

'There was young Paddy Reilly, now, it was on the parish outing that he got off with old Maggie Brennan's girl, Aisling. He'd been havering about for weeks before, like a demented hen, trying to get up the nerve, and that was the day he finally did the trick. But mind you, I don't think he'd have got anywhere with her if it hadn't been for Oonagh Laverty's new short skirt.

It was one of those short skirts that was just coming into fashion about then, and Oonagh was the first of the young girls to make an appearance in one. The fellas were struck all of a heap, and the rest of the girls were raging at Oonagh for beating them to the draw, as you might say.

As for all the old hens, they were saying Oonagh was a disgrace, going round with a skirt as short as that, but, mind you, they weren't saying it in front of big Annie Laverty, Oonagh's Ma. Annie was queening it round, as pleased as punch with all the attention her wee Oonagh was getting.

Well, as I said, the girls were right and annoyed at Oonagh, and none of them more so than Aisling Brennan, who was used to being a bit before the rest of them when it came to fashion, for her Mammy served behind the counter in W.J. Byrne's, the big drapers in Donegal Town, and she kept Aisling well up to date with all the latest styles. So, dear, didn't Aisling take it into her head to do something about it?

Well, the bus from McFarland's that had been hired for the day was sitting waiting, and up we all got. It was to take us away along the coast to where there was a nice bit of beach for the kids to do their running about, and a hall was organised for us to have our tea, or in case it would rain.

When we were all stowed in our seats, Father Donegan went the rounds giving everybody their paper bag with a bun and two sandwiches and a bit of cake, and warning the children that if they ate it now, there wouldn't be any more to have with their lemonade when we got to the hall.

5 The Parish Outing

'Dear save us, man, have you not got a titter of wit?' old Sadie Rafferty called out to him. She never cared what she said to anyone, priest or not. 'Sure you know fine the kids'll have it scoffed before the bus gets started.'

But Father Donegan paid no attention to her, that being the sort of him, though any creature with all their marlies could have told him she was right.

It was a great trip, with everybody bantering everybody else, and having a good laugh.

Then we came to a bend in the road and drove round it, and there was the sea, fresh and blue and sparkling, and enough to lift your heart out of your body. A day to make you forget everything and just jump for joy.

By the time we got down to the beach, Oonagh Laverty's skirt was forgotten about by everyone but Aisling.

What she was up to none of us rightly knew, but she disappeared away behind some bushes, and when she came out, you'd have sworn she'd got herself dressed up in a short skirt just like Oonagh's. It was only when you looked at her twice that you could see where she'd hitched her dress up someway, so it would look like one.

And, mind you, it was well for Aisling that her Ma hadn't been able to get off from the shop to come, for if she'd seen Aisling showing her legs to all and sundry that way, she'd have had the skin off her when she got her home.

It had only been the Sunday before that Father Donegan had been preaching against the same short skirts at Mass, and Maggie Brennan, not being like Sadie Rafferty, was always a great one for doing what the priest said.

Paddy Reilly couldn't take his eyes off Aisling, and he wasn't the only one, for Aisling was always a right nice looking young girl. Young Donal Neilly, and Liam O'Connell, were making up to her rightly, and I felt very sorry for poor Paddy, for he didn't seem to be able to get next nor near Aisling, at the start of it.

The sun was out and shining, and the youngsters were running along the beach and climbing the rocks. Father Donegan had his work cut out for him, getting them lined up for the racing. All most of them wanted was to get their mammies to roll up their trousers for them, if they were boys, or tuck up their frocks in their knickers, if they were girls, so they could go careering off down the beach and into the water for what they called a paddle – though with the splashing and shrieking that went on, it was more like a bear garden than anything else.

Before too long, Father Donegan had enough sense to give it up as a bad job, and he came and threw himself down beside me on the sand, where I was getting my own trousers rolled up.

'It's enough to fair sicken you, Seamus,' he started, 'after all the work I put into this, getting the spuds for the egg and spoon races and all.'

But I wasn't for listening to Father Donegan moaning much longer.

'Sure, Father, it would do your heart good to see the childer enjoying themselves on a nice day like this, and the bigger ones too, foreby!'

I was looking round for young Aisling Brennan, while I was speaking, and it was then I caught on that she wasn't anywhere in sight.

Well, there was nothing to that, and she could have gone off for a dander with one of the young fellas, or maybe had to go up to the hall for something.

I went down to the water and had my paddle, and then I sat down by the rocks and twiddled my toes in the nearest pool to see if I could find a crab, and had a bit of a crack with some of the womenfolk, and it must have been a right while after that I noticed Paddy Reilly with a face on him that would have turned buttermilk.

Now, I've always been fond of Paddy, and, sure, if things had gone different I could have been his Da, for me and Katie Maguire used to go together before she took up with Micky Reilly.

'Boys a dear, Paddy, what's eating you?' I asked him.

'Ah, nothing,' says Paddy. 'You haven't seen Aisling Brennan about, Seamus, have you?'

'Listen, Paddy,' says I, 'you catch yourself on! If you're keen on the girl, away you go and find her and make sure you cut those other boyos out! You'll get nowhere moping and moaning about that way.'

Well, for some reason, Paddy brightened up a bit at that.

'Okay, Seamus,' he said. 'You're a wise man, and I'll take your advice. I'm away off now to find her and sort things out.'

There was a look on his face that had me a bit worried, and off he charged across the beach and away up into the sand hills out of sight.

Well, he told me afterwards that he got the idea into his head that it was now or never, and it was high time Aisling Brennan got a

5 The Parish Outing

bit of sense. She'd been blowing hot and cold on him for weeks past, and he reckoned it was time she let him know where he stood.

He'd been half expecting to find her in among the sand dunes with Liam O'Donnell or one of those boys, and he was all set for having it out with her once and for all. But there wasn't hide nor hair of her to be seen, nor of any fella either.

So then he heard a sort of huffing and puffing noise coming from somewhere, and after a while he made out that it seemed to be coming from behind this big thorn bush.

Well, round the bush went Paddy, dying to know the ins and outs of whatever might be going on, and when he got to the back of the bush, sure he could hardly keep from roaring with laughter at the sight.

There was Aisling, red in the face, and near enough to bawling her eyes out, and the dress all caught up round her someway till it was near to choking the life out of her, and so badly tangled on the thorn bush that Aisling couldn't get moving for love nor money.

'Ah, Aisling, you're a sight for sore eyes!' says Paddy, trying to keep his face straight. 'Dear save us, girl, what have you been up to?'

'Will you come and give me a hand, Paddy Reilly, you great lump!' says Aisling, not knowing whether to laugh or cry. 'Do you not see I'm all caught up like a tinker's pack?'

'Sure, I can see that well enough, Aisling,' says Paddy, 'but how you managed it is what I don't see.'

At that Aisling began to bawl in real earnest. 'It was my skirt, Paddy. It was starting to slip down again where I had it hitched up, and I thought I'd just get away quiet like, behind the bushes, and fix it up again. But the old thorns kept sticking into me, and the belt got caught, and with twisting round to get it out I got more stuck, and now my good dress's getting all torn, and the mammy'll murder me when she sees it, and I don't know what to do!'

'Ah, now, Aisling, shut your gob and hold your guldering and give us a chance to get at you,' says Paddy, 'and I'll have you out of there in no time.'

So then he started tugging and hauling at the dress, but, sure as goodness, the more he tugged and hauled, the worse stuck it seemed, till in the end Paddy gave it a fierce tug and there was an almighty ripping noise and Aisling Brennan let a squeal out of her you'd have heard in Donegal Town.

The Seanachie: Tales of Old Seamus – *Gerry McCullough*

'Paddy, Paddy, what'll I do? You've ripped my dress, you hellion. How am I to get home now, with no clothes on my back?'

'Now, Aisling,' says Paddy, 'it's not as bad as all that. It's just a small tear, and sure a blind man on a galloping horse would never notice it.'

And with that, Aisling went for him with both fists flying, and Paddy had to grab her by the wrists to save himself, and over they both went into the thorn bushes.

It didn't take Paddy long to see they'd both be best out of there. He had a good hold on Aisling's wrists still, and he was right and quick off the mark, rolling him and Aisling over and away from the thorns, before they'd got more than a start made at getting themselves cut to pieces.

So there they were lying all tangled up on the sand.

And Paddy says to me, 'Seamus,' he says, 'I don't think I'll ever understand women,' for, dear to goodness, if Aisling didn't look up at him and start laughing fit to burst.

So then, Paddy said, it just seemed like a good idea for him to start kissing her.

Well, there's not much more to the story.

It was a right while later when the pair of them appeared back down on the beach, and Aisling was well covered up in Paddy's plastic raincoat, that he'd brought folded up in his pocket in case it poured. And he told me he'd promised Aisling he'd explain to her Mammy that the accident to the dress was all his fault, seeing as how he'd tripped over his own feet and knocked her flying into the thorns.

'And if there's a cheep out of her, you just refer her to me,' says he to Aisling.

As if one word out of old Maggie wouldn't have had him haring for the next county!

But there, Aisling didn't seem to be worried, walking round for the rest of the outing with her hand in Paddy's, and looking like the cat that swallowed the cream, so she must have reckoned she'd come out of the day with a good bargain.

And I suppose there's many a one would say she was right, and to end up getting a decent lad like Paddy, it would be worthwhile getting at least one dress ripped off your back!'

6 The Singing Dog

I had come up to Ardnakil in Donegal for my Christmas break, and the snow lay thickly outside as I relaxed by the glowing fire in the tumbledown little cottage belonging to my old friend Seamus O'Hare.

Outside the wind roared, but inside all was warmth and comfort, and I sighed contentedly as I stretched out my feet to the snug turf fire, backed up with a few enormous sweet smelling logs, which roared in their turn, matching the wind outside, and threw out a pleasant, beguiling heat.

'This is the life, Seamus!' I said, sipping the hot whiskey Seamus had pressed upon me when I had staggered in, frozen and powdered with snow, like some Arctic traveller of the wilds, half an hour ago. 'No wonder you chose to live here all the year round.

As a child, I, too, had lived in Ardnakil, but long since I had moved away, and now I returned only for the occasional, brief visit.

'Ah, it has its ups and downs!' said Seamus comfortably. 'Will you be staying long, Jamie? The Christmas concert, now? Will you still be about for that?'

'I hope so, Seamus,' I said. 'I'll be here over Christmas. Is it before that?'

'Indeed, it falls on the day before Christmas Eve this year,' Seamus told me. 'And in general it's an occasion I look forward to. Many's the good evening's crack I've had at these same concerts in past years.'

'Oh?' I inquired lazily, stretching out more comfortably in the deep armchair. 'That sounds like the beginning of a story.'

'Well, it could be, for that,' said Seamus with a mischievous twinkle. 'There was one year in particular, you'd maybe like to hear tell of.

'I wasn't that old, myself, at the time I'm thinking of. Not much more than a youngster. They were still trying to make me go to school. But, there, I was never much of a one for sitting in a stuffy classroom on a glorious summer's day, when the fish were rising in the cool brown pools. Or on a crisp autumn morning, with the potatoes ready for digging, and a pretty penny to be earned for my help. Or even in the depth of winter, when my bed was warm and snug, and there was snow to be hurled as snowballs at my friends, or shovelled off the garden paths for sixpence from those who could afford it, or free for those who couldn't, but who would pay me with a warm seat by the fire and a piece of home-made soda bread, warm off the griddle, for my services!

So it happened that, instead of sitting at my school desk this winter's day, I was hanging round the hall where they were rehearsing for the Christmas concert, trying not to make myself too obvious, in case I should be chased.

And that was how I first came to hear of Danny Kilpatrick, and his singing dog.

Danny was a little shrimp of a man, with a weather beaten face and a white beard.

He had come up from the south, and it seemed that he had travelled far and wide, and made his living in a way that was strange to me, youngster as I was.

He was the owner of a black and white collie, the sort that might be used for herding the sheep, but, as I heard from the chatter that was going on, a far cleverer dog than would be needed for that.

'Ah, you've never seen the like of my Bob for cleverness,' Danny was saying when I first heard him. 'He's worth every penny of his keep to me, for folks will pay me a right fistful of coins just to hear him perform. He has a fine sweet voice, and has brought tears to the eyes of many a one before now.'

'You don't say, now!' replied Declan O'Brady, the head of the local council, and he that was running the Christmas concert that year. 'And how would he do that, tell me, Danny?'

'Why, Bob can sing as well as a Christian!' retorted Danny Kilpatrick. 'Would you like to hear him?'

There was a great noise of excitement. Maggie Brennan cried out, 'Sure, who'd believe it?' but wee Jamie Halligan was shouting, 'Go on, Bob, let's hear you!' and Dominic Murphy burst out singing himself in his excitement.

Declan got them all quieted down at last, and he said to Danny, 'Well, let's have the proof of the pudding, Danny. Can he give us a good Christmas song?'

6 The Singing Dog

I could see the grin splitting Danny Kilpatrick's cheeks, even under the big white beard.

'Now, Declan,' he said, 'the dog is my livelihood. We don't perform for free, I have to tell you. But fill the hat rightly, and I'll see what Bob can do for you.'

With that, he took off his old tweed cap, and laid it solemnly on the ground before the crowd of them, and winked at Bob.

There was a bit of hesitation, but then old Tommy Reilly started the ball rolling with a half a crown thrown into the cap, and then the copper and silver followed fast from all directions. These were the days before the change in the money, you realise.

When Danny felt that there was enough in the cap to be worth his while, he set up the act.

First of all, he waved the crowd back a bit, to leave the dog plenty of room. Then he called Bob forward, and set him up, sideways on to the crowd, and took up his own position facing the dog, but with his back more than half turned towards the audience. Then he turned towards them and bowed.

'Ladies and gentlemen. As seen by all the crowned heads of Europe!' he announced impressively. 'Bob the singing dog! Has anyone a favourite request?'

'White Christmas!' called out Jamie Halligan before anyone else could get their wits together.

'White Christmas it is!' called out Danny Kilpatrick. With that he turned back to face the dog, with his back three quarters to the audience again. 'Now, Bob. Off you go!'

A moment latter there was the sound of 'White Christmas' echoing through the hall, in a high tenor voice that was, indeed, as Danny had said, sweet enough to draw tears from the hardest.

Now, as I've said, I was only a youngster myself at this time, and still innocent in many ways, hard as you may find it to believe that. Bob sat there, opening and shutting his mouth in time as the notes poured out. I gaped like the rest of them, and would have been as ready as Jamie Halligan to swear that Bob had as beautiful a voice as any I'd ever heard.

There was a deep silence when the singing was over, then, when the sound stopped, they were quiet. A moment later the clapping burst out. There were bravos, and hurrahs, and shouts of 'More! More!'

The Seanachie: Tales of Old Seamus – *Gerry McCullough*

'Ah, Danny!' exclaimed Declan O'Brady, 'I've never heard the like of it! Your Bob has the most amazing voice! It's no wonder the Kings and Queens of Europe think so highly of him!'

'Ah, now, thank you, Declan!' beamed Danny.

'Can I ask you something, Danny?'

'Ask away, Declan!'

'Would you consider getting Bob to sing for our Christmas concert, this year?'

Danny Kilpatrick smiled happily.

'Bob's always happy to sing, Declan,' he said. 'But, there, as I was saying, we have our livelihood to get. If you and I can come to a reasonable agreement about the payment, now?'

'I don't think there'll be any problem about that, Danny!'

And with that, Danny and Declan went off into a huddle together, at the far side of the hall, and they must have come to an arrangement quickly, for when they came back, they were both beaming all over their faces.

'It'll be the best Christmas concert ever!' exclaimed Declan O'Brady, his face all smiles 'I couldn't have believed it, if I hadn't heard it, myself.'

I had dodged away behind the curtain by now, having no great desire to be chased off to school by Declan O'Brady or anyone else. Presently I saw Danny and Bob heading off back to the small cottage where they were lodging with old mother O'Donnell.

I was curious enough to want to follow them home.

I would know better now, I suppose.

It's not right, I know, to listen in to a conversation that's not meant for your ears.

But, sure, I was just a youngster then, and I have to admit I went quietly up to the window. It was getting dark already, with the short winter days.

There was light streaming out from the cottage windows, for Danny hadn't thought to draw the curtains.

I leaned up against the window, being careful to keep to one side, out of sight, and I listened.

'Ah, Bob' Danny was saying, 'Where would I be without you? Starving in a ditch, I suppose! Maybe what I'm doing's wrong, but what alternative have I?

6 The Singing Dog

'It's the clever wee dog you are, whatever they may say!'

Then I saw Danny, leaning back beside the fire, with Bob's head in his lap, and I heard him begin to sing.

What I heard was a lovely pure, tenor voice, the likes of John McCormick, and I tell you, it brought the tears to my eyes, youngster though I was. There was no pretence, this time, that it was Bob doing the singing. Danny sang his heart out, while I listened, then he sat up, wiped his eyes, and said, in a natural voice,

'Right, Bob, time for your supper. Though why they won't pay me a living wage for singing, though they'll pay you, I'll never understand. Come on, boy!'

He went off to the kitchen, to put out Bob's dog food, and I took the opportunity to slip off quietly into the darkness.

It was a few days later, when I was mitching off school again, that I saw Danny and Bob walking through the fields. I've always been interested in people – nosy, some folks would say. I don't see it that way, myself. Anyhow, I dandered along in the same direction, far enough back to be out of sight.

Danny was walking across old Trevor McGonnigal's fields, and on into his woods. I knew old McGonnigal was a man for the traps, not wanting any poachers to take his young pheasants. Many a bird I've taken from him myself, for all that, over the years. I knew enough, you understand, to be able to avoid any of his traps easily. It was clear, from the careless way he was walking, that Danny had no idea of the risk he was taking in walking there.

I was debating in myself if I should warn him, when it happened.

Bob had been running ahead, then circling back to his master, then running ahead again, as is the way of all dogs, when suddenly, I realised that it was too late. There was an almighty howl, then Danny sprang forward.

Bob had been caught in a trap!

I darted out from behind the bushes.

'Quick!' I ordered brusquely. 'If you want to save his leg, hold on to this part of the trap. I need both hands to prise the teeth free.'

I gritted my jaw, put all my strength into it, and pushed the horrible teeth of the trap apart.

'Pull his leg out!' I ordered. 'I can't hold on much longer.'

Danny, his face white, obediently pulled Bob's leg clear.

The Seanachie: Tales of Old Seamus – *Gerry McCullough*

With a gasp of relief, I relaxed my muscles, and the trap snapped shut again.

Bob was a big, heavy dog. Neither Danny nor I was that big or strong. We wouldn't be able to carry him.

I took in the situation.

'Right,' I said. 'I'll need to fetch help. You look after him, and keep him warm, above all. I'll be back as quick as I can.'

On the word, I took off across the fields, and headed like an arrow for the nearest farm, Declan O'Brady's.

It wasn't that long before we were back with a couple of farm hands and a bit of fencing to carry Bob to the vet.

But when I got back, I noticed that Danny had taken off his coat to wrap around his dog, and that he was shivering, and probably had been shivering for some time.

'Get home, Danny, and have a hot drink,' I advised him. You don't want to risk a cold.'

But Danny hardly listened to me, for he was more concerned with Bob than with anything else. Instead of going home to the warm, he trotted along beside the two men as they carried Bob on the fencing, all the way to the vet, and hung around outside while the vet, Mr. Armstrong, put ointment on Bob's leg, bandaged it up, and finally pronounced that he could be taken home now.

I called round to see Danny a few days later.

Bob was fine. Mr. Armstrong had told Danny not to worry about the sore leg for he expected it to heal up quickly.

But Danny was a different matter.

He was sitting by the fire, wrapped in a blanket, and he was coughing.

I listened to him, and I have to say that I was worried.

It was three days to the Christmas concert.

Declan O'Brady was calling round at Danny's regularly, worried if Bob would be able to carry out his contract.

I was on the spot a couple of times, and I heard Danny assure him that there would be no problem, that Bob's leg wouldn't affect his singing voice, and that everything would be okay.

I heard Danny cough and wheeze as he said it, and I wondered.

The evening of the concert came round.

6 The Singing Dog

I had sneaked in behind the stage, not having enough money to pay for a ticket. I crouched down behind a hamper of stage properties, and I watched the various acts.

There was Megan Devine, singing 'music hall hits of yesteryear', and getting a big hand for it.

Then there was big Simon, the butcher, doing his turn with the comic stuff that he'd pinched from the radio.

Dominic Murphy held them with his farmyard imitations, and Peter O'Hara got a good round of applause for his speeches from Shakespeare.

Then Declan O'Brady, who was doing compere, stood up and introduced Danny Kilpatrick and his singing dog.

Such a build up as he gave him.

You would have thought there had never been anything seen or heard of like Bob and his beautiful tenor voice in the whole world before.

And, suddenly, there they were.

Bob, his leg still bandaged.

But otherwise fine, as far as you could tell.

And Danny, sitting half facing his collie, a funny look on his face, not really visible to the audience, but clear enough to me where I crouched behind the big hamper in the wings.

The piano, played by Aisling Donahue, who was more used to the organ on Sunday to tell the truth, started up.

It was *'White Christmas',* as before.

Bob didn't sound just as good as he had done when I'd heard him at the practice, I couldn't help thinking. Still and all, he got through to the end of the tune with a lot of applause, for all that.

Then it was time for a few Christmas carols.

The first one was 'Silent Night'.

I listened as Bob struck up the first few notes.

The first line was perfect.

Then, suddenly, it wasn't just so good.

There was a bit of gasping, and wheezing.

Then a few good notes, then a fit of coughing, and then it seemed that Bob had struck some problem, and found it hard to go on.

There was a silence, mixed with a few coughs.

Bob was still opening and closing his mouth, as Danny must have trained him to do.

The Seanachie: Tales of Old Seamus – *Gerry McCullough*

A muttering began to run round the hall.

'What's the problem?'

'Sing up, there, Bob!'

I could see Danny's face, from my vantage point behind the hamper.

He looked suddenly desperate.

I knew what had happened. In his care for his dog, he had allowed himself to catch cold, and now he had lost his voice.

Danny looked helplessly around the hall.

I could see the despair in his eyes.

Then, suddenly, the notes rang out again.

'Sleeps the world, hid from sight,'

There was silence throughout the hall.

The high, clear voice continued until the end of the carol.

There was a thunderstruck pause.

Then, first a faint pattering, then a bit more. Then, with a sound like thunder, the applause broke out.

People were standing, clapping wildly, shouting out 'More! More!', stamping their feet.

Danny stood up, bowing modestly.

When, at last, the applause died down enough to allow him to speak, he said, 'Ladies and gentlemen! Bob and I want to thank you, very sincerely, for your appreciation. You have to realise that this performance, this singing, takes it out of Bob. I'm sorry, but that must be all for tonight.'

He looked around him. It's true to say that there wasn't a dry eye in the house.

'If any of you ladies and gentlemen,' he added, slyly, 'would like to show your appreciation in the usual way, there will be a cap by the doorway for your contributions.'

I don't know how much extra Danny made that night. Enough, I would guess, to keep him and Bob in comfort until the better weather, when Danny's throat would be well again.

I slipped out of the hall by the back way before anyone noticed me, and made my way home.

It had been an interesting night. I had enjoyed myself. It had been fun.

There had been one nervous moment, though.

The moment when I had wondered if my voice would hold out for that last high note in 'Silent Night'.

7 The Cuckoo Clock

I had come up to the little Donegal village of Ardnakil for a few days break, as I often did. When I walked round on the first evening to *The Golden Pheasant*, looking to meet up with some of my friends, and have a bit of craic over a pint, I saw Seamus O'Hare sitting at the bar, smoking his foul old pipe and looking pretty contented.

I've known Seamus since I was a child visiting my grandparents in Ardnakil, and it was always a pleasure to see him.

We greeted each other warmly, and were just settling down for a chat, when our first words were interrupted by a loud, 'Bong! Bong! Bong!'

I looked round in surprise, and realised that the sound had come from the clock on the wall behind us. As I watched, a wooden bird on a spring emerged suddenly from an opening door on the front, and I heard the repeated, 'Cuckoo! Cuckoo!' Eight times.

'I didn't know anyone had a cuckoo clock these days, Seamus!' I exclaimed.

'Oh, there are still some about,' Seamus said comfortably. 'Some like them, and some don't. My friend Liam O'Hanlon, now, he's one can't stand the crayters. I could tell you a story about that, if you'd like to hear it.'

'Fire away there, Seamus,' I said, and I settled myself comfortably to listen.

'Well, now,' Seamus said, 'this is the story as Liam told it to me.

'The wind was howling like a banshee flying fiercely across the dark sky.

The moon glimmered and flickered through gaps in the clouds that were scurrying through the stormy night like lost sheep.

The Seanachie: Tales of Old Seamus – *Gerry McCullough*

The moonlight was doing its best to light up the wet grass, the sleeping flowers, the muddy, rutted lane under Katie's and Liam's feet, but sure it wasn't having much success.

Liam had a strange eerie feeling that someone was laughing at them.

What in the name of goodness, he wondered, was he doing letting Katie talk him into this nonsense?

They moved forward cautiously on tip-toe, and when they reached the garden gate it creaked as Liam pushed it open.

All around them, the trees shook their branches angrily, with a great rustling of leaves, as if to inquire what they thought they were doing there. High up, an owl shrieked and came swooping in front of Liam's face.

The night was full of strange and frightening sounds.

But for all its wildness, it was amazingly beautiful.

Liam was peering up at the sky, trying to identify the few stars he could see, when Katie's voice sounded abruptly in his ear.

'Man dear, Liam O'Hanlon, will you get a move on, standing there like a stuck pig?'

Liam jumped a mile or so with terror.

'Dear sakes, Katie, get a grip on yourself! No need to scare the living daylights out of a man!'

His words sounded weak because of the need to whisper.

'The longer we wait here, the more likely we are to be spotted!' Katie said. Her jaw was thrust forward in determination, her mouth pursed up in a tight, forceful line. Very familiar.

Liam had been looking at that expression, or something like it, for most of his life.

Though he told me he didn't remember ever noticing it before the day they were married, or he might have had second thoughts, maybe.

He turned his eyes away from the night sky, and looked instead at the closed doors and windows of the house.

'Well, now, Katie,' he said. 'I don't quite see how you mean to get in, with everything being locked up?'

Liam's a reasonable man, and he spoke reasonably, keeping to himself how daft he thought the whole carry-on was.

'How I mean to get in, Liam O'Hanlon?' Katie echoed angrily. 'It's you that's supposed to get in, that is if you're a man at all! I'll come

7 The Cuckoo Clock

after you, if it seems simple enough. Now, get on with it, and open one of them windows. Sure, it'll be easy!'

They made their way up the winding garden path, still tripping over things in the darkness, until the bulk of the empty house loomed up over them.

Katie nudged Liam sharply with her elbow. He saw he would have to make a start.

He had his old penknife in his pocket, and he reached up to the nearest window, to try if he could force the catch.

But as he told me, the last thing it was, was easy.

He was puffing and panting and his arms were right and sore from stretching up, when he felt something give. A moment later there was an almighty screech as the sash went shooting upwards.

He pushed it as far as it would go, then he got his knee on the window sill, and on headfirst into the room.

Katie was dancing with impatience down below. Liam turned and leaned out, to give her a hand up.

Give her this, he thought, she was agile enough at the climbing up, her being a thin bit of a woman, and having had the wit to wear a pair of trousers for the job.

He soon had her up and standing beside him.

'Listen, now, Katie, do you not think we should give up on this and go home?' he begged. He was shivering and hugging his arms round him, and not with the cold, I'm telling you. 'Suppose somebody catches us here where we've no right to be?'

'No right? Haven't I every right to be in my dead sister Nuala's house?' demanded Katie.

'Sure, Katie, it's your niece Roisin's house now, and if Roisin had thought you had a right to be in it, wouldn't she have given you a key?' Liam asked rashly.

Even in the patchy moonlight he could see the glare Katie gave him, enough to make the hairs on your chest stand on end.

He'd been fool enough to start her off again.

'All I want is my rights,' she hissed at him. 'My mammy's cuckoo clock was to come to me after Nuala, the mammy always said so. And now Nuala's gone, and no sign of that skitter of a Roisin ever giving me what's rightfully mine! Well, I'm not one to make a fuss, but if she thinks she can treat me like this she's got another think coming.'

The Seanachie: Tales of Old Seamus – *Gerry McCullough*

The moonlight glittered on her eyes. She darted forward and gave him a shove.

'Come on there, you great lump! Mammy's clock'll be in the parlour. That's where Nuala kept it, the one and only time she ever invited me to her house, and her my own sister.'

Liam could have said something, but he had the sense to keep his mouth shut. If Katie hadn't had such a flaming row with her sister on that one and only occasion, she might have been asked back. Sure, nobody likes to be told to her face that she's well rid of her husband, and him only recently dead. That he was a lazy good-for-nothing git, who sponged off Nuala all her life. And moreover, that Roisin took after her Da, and had legs like tree trunks into the bargain.

And, mind you, Katie could never be made to see that she'd spoken out of turn. 'I speak as I find,' was all she would say. 'If folks don't like to hear the truth, it's their look-out.'

She was over trying the door-handle by this time.

They were in the kitchen, a big, gloomy place with a lot of dust and some remains of food still around.

Roisin, who worked in Dublin, clearly hadn't found time yet to clear the place up, and sure, Nuala had been too ill the last few weeks to do much. No need for Katie to turn her nose up at it, Liam thought.

There was a scuffling sound from under the big dresser. Mice, Liam thought, or maybe even rats.

Katie suddenly noticed the scuffling and scratching, and let out a shriek.

'Dear save us, what is it?'

'Ghosts,' Liam suggested helpfully, knowing how Katie felt about even mice.

Then he wished he hadn't made the suggestion.

The branches of the trees outside were making weird moving shadows on the kitchen walls, and it was as much as he could do to keep assuring himself that trees it was, and nothing else.

Suddenly a shrill sound had him jumping out of his skin.

It was just Katie opening the door, which for sure needed oiling. The moment she had it open she was out of there with a bound.

'Ghosts my foot!' she snorted. 'Come on, man dear, this here's the parlour door.'

They tiptoed on down the hallway.

7 The Cuckoo Clock

The parlour door was tight shut. At first Liam couldn't see how they could open it.

Katie shoved him out of the way.

'Do you not see the key sticking out of the lock, Liam O'Hanlon? Sure, the parlour was always kept locked, with all the fancy ornaments the mammy had in it.'

She twisted the key and pushed the door open, and away in and over to the far wall where the cuckoo clock was hanging.

In a second she had it down and was crooning over it like it was a baby.

'Let's be out of here, Katie!' Liam urged her, pulling at her arm.

All of a sudden there was a whirring sound and then, 'Bong! Bong! Bong!'

'Heavens, what the dear sakes is it?' Liam shouted, before he could stop himself.

Then right in his ear, 'Cuckoo! Cuckoo! Cuckoo!'

It was the blasted clock telling everyone in earshot it was three o'clock!

Katie was just as terrified as Liam was, whatever she told him afterwards.

Then no sooner had they got back their breath than something else happened.

From the back of the house they heard a loud snarling, screeching sound, echoing round the empty house as if all the devils in hell were on the warpath and coming after Katie and Liam!

Katie grabbed Liam's arm and nearly dropped the clock, and as for Liam, he was grabbing her at the same time.

Then they both came to their senses and bucketed down the hallway towards the open kitchen window.

They belted through the kitchen, the awful noise behind them getting louder all the time, and whether Liam would have been a gentleman and let Katie go first, who knows, but with a scurry and a shove she was past him and taking a header out the window, hugging the clock, leaving Liam still flung against the kitchen table.

There was a shrill sort of a racket coming from whatever was under the dresser. Liam wasn't for waiting to see what fearsome boggart might be coming after them. He clambered onto the window ledge. He could hear the thump of something huge skidding across the kitchen floor.

The Seanachie: Tales of Old Seamus – *Gerry McCullough*

He risked a quick look round.

An enormous shadow followed him the length of the kitchen wall.

'It's the Hound of the Baskervilles!' he shouted.

Then, as he leapt from the window, he felt sharp teeth clashing together on the seat of his trousers, and a pain that didn't come from any ghost.

He staggered after Katie, who was away off down the lane by now, screeching at the top of her voice.

'It's all right, Katie!' he panted out as he followed her as best as he could for the pain in his rear-end. 'There's nothing to be scared of! It's only Nuala's old dog!'

The next afternoon there was a knock on the door, and there was Katie's niece Roisin.

Katie sent Liam to answer it, while she hid the clock under the sofa.

'Come in, child dear,' she said, being over friendly for fear Roisin had come to demand the clock back. 'Come and sit down.'

Roisin sat down on the sofa. The cuckoo clock was just under her feet.

'Oh, Auntie Katie,' she said, looking upset, near to tears. 'I don't know how to tell you. I've got awful bad news for you.'

Katie couldn't utter a word.

'You know my Granny's cuckoo clock?' Roisin said. 'My mammy always said you were to have it when she was gone. I promised her I'd make sure you got it. I haven't had a chance to sort things out until today. I arranged to take this week off work and tidy up the house and that. But, oh, Auntie, when I went round this morning, hadn't some right hallion's broken in and stole my mammy's good clock! I don't know what else they took. Old Growler interrupted them and scared them off, but, oh, auntie! I'd rather they took anything else than your clock!'

She burst into tears.

'There's one thing,' she went on, 'one of them got a good bite, for Growler had a bit of cloth caught on his teeth, and I'm thinking the Guards could match it up to the tear in the rascal's trousers.'

Liam had been choosing to stand up that day rather than sit. At Roisin's words, he shuffled himself round a bit, to make sure the rip in his trousers was better hidden.

7 The Cuckoo Clock

Katie still hadn't spoken. Maybe she was thinking of what she'd gone through last night, for a clock she'd have got anyway. And one that she'd have to spend the rest of her life hiding, in case Roisin got to hear that she had it after all.

It was coming up to four o'clock.

From under the sofa came the sound Katie and Liam had heard it in the parlour at Nuala's.

Bong! Bong! Bong! Bong!

Roisin's eyes got rounder and rounder as she stared at Katie.

Katie's face got redder and redder.

From under Roisin's feet at the edge of the sofa, they heard the cuckoo clock striking the hour –

'Cuckoo! Cuckoo! Cuckoo! Cuckoo!'

It seemed that Liam had been right. Someone must have been laughing at them all along.'

8 The Mill Pool

One pleasant spring day, I set out to climb the green, rocky hill which rises behind the small, white-washed cottage in the little Donegal village of Ardnakil, where I had been coming, for many years now, whenever I badly needed rest and relaxation from my city job.

It was an easy enough climb. I could manage it with just enough effort to feel that I was getting some healthy exercise, without overdoing it.

The sun was shining, the sky was fresh and clear, and hearts-ease, daisies, primroses, even a few stray violets, the little wild spring flowers, were scenting the air delicately.

I hummed to myself light-heartedly as I climbed higher, and when I finally reached the top, I threw myself down on the soft spring grass and looked round me with great pleasure.

I could see in all directions for mile upon mile. To one side, the peak of Mount Errigal thrust its distinctive point upwards. Much further to the West I could just catch the sparkle of white waves on the deep blue Atlantic. Directly below me was my own friendly cottage, and, nearby, Ardnakil village, spread out like a coloured picture book for my enjoyment. At the further edge of the village, beside the river, I could see the old mill, no longer working, alas, and the pretty mill pond beside it, with the leafy green trees and bright flowering plants which edged its banks. Shafts of sunlight glinted off its calm surface.

I lay on my stomach and looked my fill, with an indescribable satisfaction, and as I lay there, the one thing missing to make it a perfect day was supplied. I heard the scrambling sound of someone else's approach. A moment later, a head appeared over the brow of the hill.

It was my old friend Seamus O'Hare.

'Seamus!' I exclaimed in delight. 'Good to see you!'

We exchanged friendly greetings, and presently I produced the packet of sandwiches and the flask of tea I had brought, and we shared them. Then Seamus pulled out his old pipe and lit up, and we leant back against a couple of handy rocks, and chatted.

'I've just been looking at the old mill, and the pool, Seamus,' I said presently. 'What a picture it makes! It's a shame it isn't used nowadays. I suppose,' I went on, 'you would remember it when it was in full working order?'

It was too good a cue for a story for Seamus to resist.

'Indeed I do, Jamie,' he said. 'It was the centre of village life, that mill, at one time. Many a thing happened there, and many a story I could tell you about it.'

I settled back, relaxing lazily, and listened.

'I suppose the most interesting of all would be the story of young Fergal MacGarry, and the way his whole life was changed by what happened to him down at the mill.

It was a beautiful Spring evening, following a day very like this one, when young Fergal went for a stroll all by himself down the old lane that still leads to the mill pool – for at this time in his life, Fergal hadn't very much in the way of friends.

Now, I'll need to tell you a bit about this same Fergal.

He was a tall, thin, gangly sort of a lad, with reddish hair and a lot of freckles, and not, to tell you the truth, the most handsome of the local boys. But that was no matter, and there were many worse looking than him.

But what had come between Fergal and the other youngsters of the neighbourhood was this, that ever since he was little, Fergal had been a born coward.

Now, I don't know what started him off being always so scared of his own shadow.

I would guess that something had frightened him badly while he was still too young to remember, but, if so, Fergal himself had no idea of what it might have been.

Anyway, the result was that if there was a tall, difficult tree to climb, and all the other boys of his age were rushing to show how well they could climb it, Fergal would be the one hanging back and keeping his feet safely on firm ground.

If there was a fierce dog in the path, Fergal would be the first to back off and go miles out of his way, rather than pass it.

If one of the local farmers was known as specially hard and crusty, and the other lads, for that very reason, took delight in slipping

8 The Mill Pool

stealthily over his walls to steal his apples, Fergal would be the one with an excuse – 'wanted at home', 'hurt his wrist' – or something that struck the other lads as equally weak, to get out of joining the raiding party.

But the climax came when the school teacher arranged a trip to a nearby castle, mostly in ruins, and while the rest of his age group were merrily jumping and climbing over the crumbling walls, Fergal, who had forced himself to climb up some rickety stairs to a broad window ledge, found, to his shame, that he couldn't bring himself to climb back down, and had to be rescued by the teacher.

So by the time he was in his early twenties, Fergal was regarded by most people in the neighbourhood as an out and out coward, and they generally left him pretty much alone.

And to be honest, there was a lot of truth in the view people had of him.

Fergal was, and always had been, someone who looked after his own skin, and believed in safety first.

So on this lovely Spring evening, his pleasure in the day was spoilt by the fact that no one had wanted to come with him on his stroll.

And in particular, Máire Murphy, a pretty little black-haired lass, who he would really have liked to get on good terms with.

Now, like everyone else, I didn't bother much with Fergal in those days, so I only heard the true facts of what happened years later, when we were sharing a chat and a pint in front of my good turf fire, one winter evening. By that time, believe it or not, Fergal and I were the best of friends, and I had long since changed my opinion of him.

On this Spring evening, then, Fergal was just coming to the last bend in the lane which led out onto the bank of the mill pond, when all of a sudden he heard a cry and a loud splashing.

He rushed round the bend straight away, and there before his eyes was a dreadful sight.

It was Máire Murphy's little sister Aine, and she was splashing and screaming and waving her arms about, in the middle of the pool.

It seemed, from the semi-hysterical cries of her mother on the far bank, that Aine had been leaning over to pick some of the flowers, strictly against her mother's firm instructions, and had toppled over. Before Mary Murphy had been able to grasp hold of her, the child had floated far beyond her reach.

The Seanachie: Tales of Old Seamus – *Gerry McCullough*

Mary's screams, added to Aine's own cries, rent the evening air, and Fergal, who had the habit of justifying as common sense what everyone else described as cowardice, thought, 'There'll be someone along in a minute who can swim better than me! No sense in both of us drowning!'

There was a small boat usually moored not far from where he was standing, and Fergal reckoned that the best thing he could do was take this boat over and try to reach young Aine from it.

He was turning away to go in search of the boat, when disaster struck.

Fergal's foot slipped on the wet grass at the edge of the pool.

Next moment, with an almighty splash, he had joined the struggling child in the water.

For want of anything else to grab at, he grabbed hold of Aine.

'Fergal, Fergal!' the child wailed, 'rescue me!'

But indeed Fergal was more concerned with being rescued himself!

He was desperately treading water and commending his soul to God when suddenly, unbelievably, he heard what sounded like loud cheering in his ears.

People had heard the screams, and come running from all directions to help.

Now, you know, and I know, for Fergal told me, just what had happened, but to the watching mother on the bank, and to the first panting arrivals, it wasn't as easy to follow as all that.

Hardly a moment had passed between Fergal's arrival at the edge, his decision to go for the boat, and his entry into the mill pond.

To the watchers, it seemed clear that what they were seeing was a heroic rescue.

And when it became clear that the rescuer himself was in difficulties, they only believed that his courage in jumping in was all the greater.

'Oh, save him, save him!' wept Mary Murphy. 'Save the brave lad, and my little Aine!'

'It's all right, Mrs. Murphy!' roared big Paddy Reilly, who by now had rushed to her side. 'We'll throw in the lifebelt, and tow them both out safely!'

8 The Mill Pool

There was a lifebelt always kept by the side of the pond, for just such situations as this, although both Mary Murphy and Fergal had forgotten all about it till that moment.

So Paddy broke the glass protecting the lifebelt, and hurled it in, keeping a good grasp on the rope, and Fergal, who as I said was always good at saving his own skin, lost no time in seizing hold of it.

And since he still had hold of little Aine with his other hand (although he told me that he had almost forgotten that he had!) the little girl was also getting enough support to keep her head above water.

So then big Paddy and some of the other lads towed the pair of them to the edge, and there were willing hands enough to take the child from Fergal's grasp, and to haul him in turn onto the bank.

Then there was shaking of hands, and much clapping of Fergal on the back, and a lot of general rejoicing and congratulation, and Fergal, who had still hardly realized what was happening, found himself, dazed and confused, being hailed as a public hero for the first time in his life!

Mary Murphy, still on the verge of hysterics, weeping and laughing by turns, was throwing her arms round first Aine and then Fergal, and hardly able to express her thanks and her gratitude in strong enough words.

At soon as she had got her wits about her, she insisted on Fergal coming home with her and the little girl to get warmed and dried – 'before you both catch your deaths of cold!' – 'I'll not take no for an answer!' she declared, with one arm round Fergal and one round Aine. 'My cottage is much the nearest. I'd never forgive myself if I let you go all the way through the village to your own home, dripping wet! And your mammy would never forgive me either!'

So Fergal, nothing loath, to tell the truth, allowed himself to be bundled along to the Murphy's cottage and put into the best chair before the fire with a couple of warm towels wrapped round him, Mr. Murphy's best coat over his shoulders, his feet in a bowl of hot steaming water, and a mug of Mary Murphy's good mutton soup in his hands.

And to crown it all, there was Máire Murphy, hovering round him anxiously, offering him more soup – 'or a drop of something stronger?' – and with her big eyes shinning like stars every time she looked at him.

The Seanachie: Tales of Old Seamus – *Gerry McCullough*

And when, later, Fergal suggested that she might like to go for a walk with him the next evening, he could hardly believe it when Máire couldn't say yes quick enough.

So it was the happiest of endings for Fergal, as you can see, and from then on, no one thought of him as a coward ever again.'

'But, Seamus,' I said. 'That's all very well, but what about the next time Fergal turned tail when he shouldn't have? Surely the people, and especially Máire Murphy, would very soon have found him out?'

'Ah, well, that's where the strange thing comes in, Jamie,' said old Seamus. 'It's to do with psychology, I reckon. From that time on, when he saw everybody regarding him as a hero, and he realized what a difference it was making to his life, Fergal managed to get himself a bit of gumption. I never saw him act the coward after that.

Fergal couldn't have explained why it should be so, himself, but there's no question that it was a fact.

Indeed, not many weeks after that, I saw the change in him with my own eyes, for he was out walking with Máire Murphy one afternoon when a great brute of a dog leapt out at the both of them, and instead of running, young Fergal took a slash at him with a big stick, and drove the brute away yelping!

I reckoned it was having Máire Murphy clinging onto his arm, relying on him and fully expecting him to save her, that made the difference.

Before long I'd come to see what a lot of good there really was in Fergal MacGarry, buried beneath his old bad habit of fear, and I was sorry I'd never tried to get to know him better before that. He did no more running away from dogs, or people, and many's the time I noticed him standing up for one of the younger boys when the bigger lads were set to tease him.

It taught me never to write anyone off like that again, without giving them a bit of encouragement to be different.

And so in the end it was me Fergal asked to be best man at his wedding, for, as I said earlier, by that time him and me had became the best of friends!'

9 At the Summer Fair

It had been one of those baking hot summer days that we get so rarely, the kind of day when you feel, guiltily, that it's almost too hot.

Guiltily, because, in our climate, we feel we should appreciate whatever hot sunny weather we get!

I was taking a short break at the cottage I had inherited from my family, in the little village of Ardnakil in Donegal, and I had spent the day lying lazily on the nearest beach, alternately roasting in the sun and splashing into the icy waters of the Atlantic, for the briefest of swims, and then out again to dry in the heat of the sun.

Now, back home, and still in that relaxed lazy mood, I decided to take a stroll round, in the cool of the evening, to see my old friend Seamus O'Hare.

I found him sitting at the side of his tumbledown old cottage, enjoying a last pipe, and listening to the sleepy chirping of the songbirds, as he took his ease in the shade of the big wild cherry, which spread its branches as high as his bedroom window.

The sky was still a lovely deep, summer blue, with only the faintest streaks of white cloud, and some pale pink and yellow remains of the recent sunset.

'Sit down, Jamie,' he greeted me. 'Sit down and smell the day. Isn't it worth smelling?'

I followed his instructions, sprawling on the rough grass beside him, and sniffing contentedly.

'That's honeysuckle,' Seamus told me. He had been my instructor in all things natural since I was a boy. 'And maybe you'll get the scent of the wild roses down the lane there? They're mostly over by now, though.'

He gave a sigh, so quiet a sigh that if the evening had not been so still I would have missed it.

The Seanachie: Tales of Old Seamus – *Gerry McCullough*

'All things pass,' said old Seamus, and I looked at him in surprise, for it isn't often that my friend Seamus is anything but cheerful, optimistic and amusing.

'Evenings like this,' old Seamus said, 'bring back the past to me. Memories of my boyhood, and of days long gone by. Happy memories, mostly.'

I sat still, saying nothing, not caring to interrupt this unusual mood, by one of my regular joking requests for a story.

'I've been sitting here,' said Seamus, 'drinking in the sounds and sights and scents of this lovely summer evening, and I've been thinking of one particular summer evening long ago.'

'Do you feel like telling me about it?' I asked quietly, at last.

'Sure, why not? And don't be worrying, Jamie, it's a happy enough story! It happened many years ago. Just about this time of year, for it was the time of the Summer Fair.'

I nodded. The annual Summer Fair was one of the year's big events at Ardnakil, and I'd been to it several times over the years, in fact had been looking forward to calling in next week, when the fair was due again.

'I needn't describe it to you,' Seamus went on. 'The roundabouts, the boat swings and chairplane swings, the stalls with everything from vegetables to the latest fashions (or so we thought them!), and the souvenirs from all over the world (though mostly stamped from China!). The amusements, from the hoopla stall to the rifle range, and the try your strength hammer. And the people! Above all, the people! The crowds who flocked in from miles around, determined not to miss a thing, dressed in their best and raring to go.

But even better, the fair people. Exotic travelling people, bright eyed, brown skinned and merry, dressed in wild, brightly coloured shirts and skirts, the like of which we quiet folks in Ardnakil had never seen before. And they joking and calling out in loud outlandish voices, with strange accents and sometimes in strange languages! It was an experience different from anything else we knew, and it thrilled my heart to be there, right from the first time I was taken along as a child, just about able to toddle.

The year I was telling you about, it had been baking hot weather, just like this spell we're having now.

9 At the Summer Fair

I was a young teenager at the time, fifteen, or would it have been sixteen? I forget, now. But just, I suppose, at a boy's most impressionable age.

I was standing by the hoopla stall, wondering whether to try my luck again. I'd already spent more than I could afford, trying for a mouth organ that had taken my fancy, and missing time after time, for the rules, written up above the stall, said that the hoopla ring had to lie flat on the table over the object, and the truth was that the stands for most of the objects were just too big to allow for that.

The stall keeper, a sulky, bad tempered looking girl, with a swarthy, spotty skin and greasy reddish hair, was very quick to point out to me my repeated failure to get the ring completely flat, and the triumphant look she had given me last time had got my back up, so that I was tempted to keep trying just for the satisfaction of finally defeating her.

She was very different from most of the fair people. I'd never seen one before who was anything but pleasant and light-hearted.

A voice spoke almost in my ear.

'Move over, Seamus O'Hare, and let someone else have a turn!'

It was Bridget Flaherty.

Bridget was a beautiful girl in her early twenties, dark haired and high coloured, with a merry twinkle in her eye, and to be honest with you, I believe I was more than half in love with her at that particular time, the sort of puppy love young boys will have for someone that bit older than themselves.

I knew rightly that she was way out of my league, but that didn't stop me day dreaming.

So Bridget paid for her hoops and began to throw, and lo and behold, her third ring landed fair and square over the bracelet she'd been aiming for! But the sulky redhead wasn't prepared to acknowledge it.

'Hard luck! Try again!' she sneered, leaning over to joggle the hoop out of position 'accidentally', with one elbow, so that now it was clearly not quite flat on the table.

Bridget Flaherty had a temper, I'll not deny.

'Why, you cheating hellion!' she cried out. 'The ring was flat until you moved it, as all these people watching can witness, and I'll thank you to give me my bracelet right now!'

The Seanachie: Tales of Old Seamus – *Gerry McCullough*

'Indeed, the ring was flat,' I supported her eagerly, and so did half a dozen bystanders, but the stall owner ignored us, and Bridget leaned over the stall towards her and made a grab at her greasy red hair.

'Give me my bracelet, you cheat!' she demanded, and she drew back her other hand, bunched up ready to punch the girl in the face, I do believe.

But just then a voice spoke behind us. A cheerful, amused voice. A voice, I could swear, that would have charmed two warring politicians into peace talks, or soothed a fractious, teething baby into sleep.

'What's all this?'

The voice belonged to a tall, vigorous young man, in the prime of his youth, clearly one of the fair people, to go by his fresh brown skin, his gleaming eyes and the white teeth that shone out when he smiled, as he was doing now.

Half a dozen voices hastened to tell him.

'What's all this, Esme?' he said again, addressing the sulky stall owner.

The girls had sprung apart on his arrival, Bridget quickly releasing her enemy's hair and Esme backing away and attempting to look calm and collected.

'I won it fair and square!' said Bridget fiercely.

'The ring isn't lying flat. You can see for yourself, Steven!' Esme wailed.

'Because you moved it, you cheating so-and-so!' Bridget flared.

Steven laughed.

Then he said, 'Now, Esme, we can't have our best customers thinking we're cheating them! Give the lady her bracelet, and we'll say no more about it!'

Then he bowed graciously to Bridget, took the bracelet from where it lay on the stall, and clasped it round Bridget's wrist with a smile that would have charmed the birds from the trees, as they say.

Esme was near to tears, I could see, but, I could also tell, she didn't want to annoy Steven.

'Take it, then,' she muttered ungraciously.

Both Steven and Bridget ignored her.

'Now, how about you and me going for a dander round the fair?' Steven asked. 'And maybe I could show you how to really enjoy the best of it?'

9 At the Summer Fair

And Bridget, blushing and smiling, seemed to me like a changed person from the forthright, strong minded girl I knew, as she went off arm in arm with the handsome traveller.

Esme scowled after them.

I was a bit young then to know much about human nature, but the look on Esme's face made me frightened. Frightened for Bridget.

It was a couple of days later that I knew that my fears were justified.

Now, don't be thinking I was eavesdropping on purpose.

But as you well know, Ardnakil's a small village, and if you enjoy strolling about it after dark, there aren't too many places where you can go, and be on your own.

So it happened that I was walking through the fields late one night, and had lain down beside a hedge to enjoy the night scents, when I realised that just on the other side of that hedge, Bridget and Steven were sitting talking.

'My mother was one of the Fair people,' Steven was saying, in a soft, ruminative voice, 'and a very beautiful girl, so I've been told. At any rate, my father, a farmer from Cork, by name Tim O'Flynn, fell in love with her at first sight. Well, she married him, and settled down as a farmer's wife. But the travelling was in her blood, and she passed it on to me, her first son, for when I reached an age to make my own choices, I left the farm to my younger brother and went with the travelling people. And so I am as you see me now, Bridget, free and happy, but without a penny to call my own.'

I missed Bridget's reply, for my attention had been seized by the sight of Esme. She was stealing quietly along beside the hedge. She didn't see me, hidden as I was by the long grasses. In her hand was a container of something white and opaque. I had no idea then what it was, though I learnt later that it was prussic acid, the sort of mixture used for killing wasps.

As I watched her in mounting fear, she crept along the hedge until she was behind Steven and Bridget.

Then, standing upright, and stretching as far as she could to reach over the high hedge towards Bridget, she uncorked the bottle, and an unpleasant smell and some smoke erupted from it.

Until then I had been frozen as still as any statue. But when I saw Esme uncork the bottle, I came to my senses.

The Seanachie: Tales of Old Seamus – *Gerry McCullough*

Leaping up from the concealing grasses, I seized the girl by both wrists, and pushed her downwards. She sank helplessly to the ground, and before anyone could interfere, the contents of the bottle had shot out and spilled far and wide over the hedge and meadow.

Esme cried out.

In a second I had my hand over her mouth, and was bundling her away beyond the sight of the couple on the other side of the hedge.

We crouched there at a distance, hidden from view, and heard their exclamations, and their final decision that it must have been a fox, or even a cat, straying nearby.

As soon as it was safe, I hauled Esme further away, and took my hand from her mouth.

She was sobbing bitterly.

'I love him! I love him!' she wept. 'Why should she have him, when I've loved him for so long?'

Suddenly I knew a fellow feeling for the wretched girl.

'And I love her, Esme,' I said quietly. 'But I don't want to destroy either her or him, all the same.'

She understood what I meant. Suddenly the whole wretched story came pouring out. She had known Steven since she was a child. The prussic acid, I learnt then, was the property of the fortune teller who travelled with the Fair, who sold love potions and death potions secretly, unknown to most of her fellow travellers. The death potion was prussic acid.

I had known that this used to happen centuries ago, but it horrified me to realise that such things still went on during my own lifetime. Esme had known of the existence of the poison, because the fortune teller had earmarked Esme as a likely inheritor of her secrets, as she herself got older.

I made Esme promise never to have anything more to do with this evil woman. So that was one good thing which came out of that night's events.

I was glad to think that since Esme had stolen the whole of her supply, it was unlikely that she would be able to acquire more, now that the laws were stricter.

'Promise you won't tell him?' Esme whispered, and I promised.

'But you must promise me never to do anything like that again.'

'I promise.'

9 At the Summer Fair

And for whatever reason, I found myself trusting her.

I realised that I felt sorry for Esme. And, since that time, I've made a point of spending some time with her every year, when the Fair came back, and was glad when a few years later she married one of the other Fair people, and lived, I think, happily, from then on.

But as for Steven O'Flynn and Bridget Flaherty?

The Fair was due to move on the next day, when I chanced to hear one final conversation between them.

It was another beautiful evening, like this, and I found myself unable to sleep.

I wandered out into the beauty of the night, and ended up, as I often did in those days, near to the Flaherty's house.

I thought sentimental thoughts of Bridget, and tried to convince myself that when Steven O'Flynn moved on with the Summer Fair, she would turn to me for comfort, and would see how much better I was in every way than Steven.

A shadowy figure emerged out of the night.

A window opened up above.

Then voices.

Steven's voice, first of all.

'Bridget!'

Bridget's voice, answering from her high window.

'It's you, Steven?'

'It's me.'

There was a brief silence.

Then Steven.

He was raising his voice in song.

I listened, awestruck.

Steven sang on. He sang a song of love, of melancholy. Of the need to love while there was still the chance.

I felt the tears trickling down my own cheeks.

Then Steven spoke.

'Bridget.'

'Yes?'

'Will you come with me, my dear? I mean to go to America, where a man can be free and where there's a chance for everyone. Will you come to me? We can marry in the church in Donegal Town, and then head across country to catch the ship from Sligo. Will you come?'

The Seanachie: Tales of Old Seamus – *Gerry McCullough*

So quietly that I almost missed it, Bridget replied.

'Yes.'

I stole quietly away in the darkness.

Next day there was an uproar.

Bridget Flaherty had disappeared.

But within a few days, the letter she had posted to her parents arrived, and the pain was reduced to the loss of a daughter across the water, rather than anything worse.

So as I told you, Jamie, it was a happy ending.

For Steven and Bridget, anyway.

The Flahertys often flew over to visit, and to see their grandchildren, for Steven made money in the New World, and could pay for their fare. And after ten years he and Bridget finally coaxed them to emigrate, and to live in a house nearby which Steven paid for.

And as for me?

I was happy for Bridget.

And for Steven, who seemed like a good person.

I never heard a bad word spoken against him, and believe me, I made it my business to inquire from the travelling people, from year to year, as they came and went.

But I think it's true to say that my heart was broken.

As much as anyone's heart can be, at fifteen.

And if you remember back to your own teenage years, I think you'll realise, that that can be quite a lot.'

10 Miracle at Ardnakil

It was one of those crisp, sunny winter days where the sky is a pale, clear blue and there is just enough of a nip in the air to be exhilarating.

I strolled in a leisurely fashion down the narrow lane which led from my little cottage in the Donegal village of Ardnakil. As I walked, I looked with pleasure at the light sprinkling of snow on the hedge tops on both sides. I was enjoying the short break I had taken from my busy city life, and I wondered how all my friends and acquaintances were getting on, and if anything had changed in the months since I had last seen them.

In particular, I wondered about my old friend Seamus O'Hare, and I hoped the cold winter weather wasn't affecting his health.

However, a few moments later, I realised that I needn't have worried, for round the corner I heard the familiar sound of his hearty chuckle, and then his voice booming out.

'Ah, now, sure this is the right sort of weather for Christmas, isn't it?'

And there he was, as hale and hearty as ever, for all his age, chatting with several of his friends in the middle of the village street.

The old street, with its cottages and shops, looked bright with Christmas lights, and there was an air of excitement and anticipation all around.

'Jamie, you're a sight for sore eyes!' Seamus exclaimed, coming towards me. 'I'm just heading home for a mug of soup, will you join me?'

I was only too pleased to accept his invitation, and ten minutes later, we were settled by the roaring turf fire in his tumble-down old cottage, nursing hot mugs of soup in our cold hands.

The Seanachie: Tales of Old Seamus – *Gerry McCullough*

As I looked round me with satisfaction, my eye was caught by a photograph propped up on the mantelpiece of a remarkably good looking young woman, red haired and as slim as a fashion model.

'Friend of yours, Seamus?' I asked casually.

'Indeed and she is!' Seamus beamed. 'I've been the best of mates with young Nora since she was so high.' He measured an impossibly small distance from the ground. 'That photo was taken a long time ago, mind you, for she's an old married woman now, and long since gone to live in America.'

I concealed my disappointment as well as I could.

'Many a tale I could tell you about the same lass!' Seamus said, 'If you're interested, that is?'

I couldn't deny that I was, for there was something very attractive about the girl in the photograph, even if it had been taken long ago.

'Nora Kilpatrick,' began Seamus, 'was left motherless when she was less than three years old. But for all that, she wasn't so badly off, for her Da, big Enda Kilpatrick, was both mother and father to the child, and indeed he couldn't have done more for her.

Enda wasn't too well off. But sure, none of us were at that time. It was one of those times, long behind us now, I'm glad to say, when there seemed to be fewer jobs than usual, and the money was getting scarcer and scarcer. Enda had a decent job at first, working for Mrs Montgomery Fitzgibbon, up at the big house, doing a bit of gardening and a bit of odd jobbing. But then, when Nora was coming ten, Mrs Fitzgibbon had to go into the nursing home, and the house was let go. So there was Enda out of a job, and getting by as well as he could with a day here and a day there, turning his hand to anything he was asked to do that would bring in an honest penny.

Nora was growing into a right pretty girl, you could see that. In a few more years, chances were she'd be a raving beauty. But though Enda did his best for her, there was no doubt he wasn't able to dress her the way the other girls of her age were dressed. She was always clean and neat, but more often than not she'd be wearing things that were far too big for her, a dress or a skirt that someone had passed on to Enda out of the goodness of their heart, but which had already had a few years' wear, and looked it.

I never heard Nora complain.

10 Miracle at Ardnakil

She knew her Daddy was doing his best for her, and if sometimes she felt bad about wearing second hand cast offs, she never showed it, or let him see.

The other children, not meaning any real harm, but kids being kids, used to make fun of her sometimes, and it was clear to me that Nora felt upset about this. But she was a bright, happy child most of the time, and that made her popular with her classmates.

Then came the time of the school Christmas party.

All Nora's friends were getting new clothes to wear to the party. The girls talked about nothing else for weeks in advance. I wouldn't say the boys were that bothered, now. But the girls thought it was the most important subject in the world.

And Nora wouldn't have been a female creature if she hadn't thought that, too.

She knew it was no use asking Enda to buy her a new dress. He would find it hard enough to manage a nicer than usual meal for Christmas day, and maybe some small present. And Nora, who was wiser than her age in money matters, wouldn't for the world have upset her father by asking for what she knew he couldn't do.

So Enda knew nothing about it, until one night, a week before the school Christmas party.

He had been working hard all day, cutting down Christmas trees and delivering them to the village shop, the last of the batch this year, and it was late enough when he came upstairs to say goodnight to his little daughter. He opened the door quietly, not wanting to wake her if she was sleeping.

But Nora was kneeling by her bed. Her eyes were closed, and he could hear her praying.

'– and, please, a new jumper for Daddy to keep him warm when he's out working. And, maybe, if it's not too much, a nice dress for me for the school party? I know it won't be a new one – but maybe one that fits properly? If it's not too much trouble? –'

Enda closed the door quietly and crept softly away.

He found it hard to keep the tears out of his eyes.

He made up his mind that whatever it took, he would get together enough money to buy a new dress for Nora. The first she would have had for years.

The Seanachie: Tales of Old Seamus – *Gerry McCullough*

Next day he set out with real determination to earn a bit of extra money by any possible means.

He went round the shops and the pubs, and asked if there was anything he could do, deliveries for the shop keepers, washing dishes at the pubs, whatever they needed.

But no one seemed to need him.

At last he was offered a few shillings by old Michael, the postman, to help out with the Christmas cards. Michael had no business trusting Enda with the mail, but, sure, Michael was getting old, and reckoned he needed a bit of help, and who was to know.

So Enda toiled round with the post, and at the end of the day, he had a few extra shillings.

But not enough, he knew, to buy Nora a dress.

He was sitting down, outside *The Golden Pheasant*, with his head in his hands, when I came across him.

'Why, Enda,' I said, 'you look as if the world's come to an end. What is it, man dear?'

And he told me all about it.

I was at a loss how to help him. I'm not so well off myself, you know, and just then, like everyone else in the country, I was worse off than usual.

All I had to offer him was my sympathy.

'There's only one thing I can do, Seamus,' said Enda finally. He sounded grim and determined. 'You know well that I'm not a gambling man. But I haven't enough here to buy the dress. I think the only thing I can do is use this money as a stake, and try to double or treble it until I have enough.'

'Ah, Enda, will you have a bit of sense!' I exclaimed. 'You're more likely than not to lose it all, and then what will you do?'

But there was no arguing with him.

That night, Enda went round to Stephen Halligan's where there was always a poker school going, and announced that he was sitting in on the game.

I went with him, for company, like, but I had more sense than to join in myself.

At first it looked hopeful.

Enda won a little, lost a little, and then won a bit more.

10 Miracle at Ardnakil

I was beginning to hope that it might work out well enough for him, but then he began to lose again, steadily.

I couldn't watch him any more.

I got up and went outside.

It seemed like only a few moments later, when Enda joined me.

'Well,' he said. 'That's that.'

'All gone?' I asked.

'All gone. I wanted to play on, on credit, but they wouldn't let me.'

'Well, thank heaven for that, anyway!' I said. 'Let's hope this will be a lesson to you, at least, Enda Kilpatrick!'

Enda looked devastated.

'I must have been mad,' he said. 'I'll never try to make money that way again. Now what am I to do?'

'Go home and have a good night's sleep,' I told him. 'Maybe in the morning you'll feel better. You might even get some work tomorrow.'

But I knew how unlikely that was.

Enda went home.

But there was no good night's sleep for him.

For hours he twisted and turned, but he could get no peace.

In the morning, he was up early, and was making the breakfast before there was any sign of life from Nora's room.

Finally she appeared, skipping happily downstairs, singing to herself.

'You seem in good form, daughter dear?' said Enda.

'Yes, I am, Daddy!' she said brightly. 'I'm looking forward to Christmas.'

Enda groaned. He felt heart broken at the disappointment coming to her.

'Nora,' he began, 'you know I'd like to give you a really nice present for Christmas, but times are hard, and I don't think I can manage much this year –'

'Ah, Daddy, don't be worrying about it!' Nora cried, throwing her arms round his neck and hugging him tightly. 'It'll all work out, just you see!' She looked at him, saw the sadness in his eyes, and spoke again.

'I didn't mean to tell you, Daddy, but you're looking so miserable I can't help it!' she said. 'I know it'll be all right, because I've been praying about it, see?'

The Seanachie: Tales of Old Seamus – *Gerry McCullough*

Enda looked at her beaming face, and felt himself near to tears. How could he bear to see his little daughter's faith destroyed?

'Nora,' he tried again.

He was interrupted by a knocking on the door.

'Who can that be?' he wondered.

It sounded like the postman. Was Michael going to ask him to help out again today? Was there going to be another few shillings, at least?

He and Nora went side by side to open the door.

Sure enough, it was the postman, Michael. In his hands was a large parcel.

'For Enda and Nora Kilpatrick,' he said. 'From America, going by the postmark. Who would that be from, now?'

'Heaven knows.'

Enda opened the parcel. Inside was a short letter.

Dear Enda,

You have probably forgotten me by now, but I feel bad about not keeping in touch. I was looking out some old photographs the other day, and I saw my sister Maureen, and I thought of you and my little niece Nora, whom I've never seen. I'm sending you a couple of presents for Christmas, with the hope that we can get back in touch again. Please write and let me know how you both are.

With love from your sister-in-law,

Eileen.

Inside were two articles wrapped in tissue paper.

The first was a warm cream coloured jumper in a man's large size.

The second was a party dress.

It was a deep, lovely blue, just the colour of Nora's eyes.

And it was exactly in Nora's size.

Enda couldn't believe it. How could this be happening?

Then he looked at Nora. Her eyes, bright and enormous, were shining with happiness.

'I told you it would be all right, Daddy, didn't I?' she said.

'Yes, pet, you did,' said Enda.

10 Miracle at Ardnakil

There was no little girl at the school Christmas party that year who looked prettier or better dressed than Nora Kilpatrick.

And there was no happier or prouder father than big Enda.

'You can say what you like, but I know what I believe. It was a pure miracle, Seamus,' he said to me, when he told me about it.

And, indeed, I believe it was.

11 Two Different Valentines

My friend Seamus O'Hare is an old bachelor, and happy to be one, or so I've always understood. But very early one February morning, when the first spring flowers were poking their heads out cautiously above the earth, and the sky was that pale, fresh, duck egg blue that tells us at once how young the year still is, I had taken a notion to rise earlier than usual, and I met him as I strolled in the fields near Ardnakil. It was then that I made a surprising discovery about him.

He was stooping over, and didn't see me approaching, and the first thing I noticed was that he had a posy of crocuses, gold and white and purple, in his hand.

I hesitated at first to interrupt him, for there was an air of secrecy about him, and he seemed wholly engrossed in his task, searching out each flower and adding it carefully to the bunch he carried in his gnarled old fist.

Then I reckoned that over the many years during which I had regularly visited the little cottage in Ardnakil, the small village set among the hills of Donegal, I had always spent time with Seamus. Surely that must count for something in the way of friendship?

I called out to him.

'Hi, Seamus! Good to see you, you old ruffian!'

He gave a startled leap in the air, and nearly dropped the flowers. Then he greeted me in turn, but with a shamefaced, hangdog air. I thought he had begun to hide the flowers behind his back. But then he must have decided that it was too late for that, and decided to brazen it out.

'Lovely flowers you have there, Seamus,' I said to him. 'Are they for someone in particular?'

Seamus' brown, wrinkled face turned pink.

'Ah, no, nobody special,' he said quickly. 'I just thought it would be nice to pick a bunch of them for myself.'

The Seanachie: Tales of Old Seamus – *Gerry McCullough*

I said nothing, but I looked at him with a quizzical expression.

Seamus laughed. 'Sure, I can't lie to you, Jamie. You've caught me out. Yes, they are for someone in particular. I suppose I'll have to tell you the whole story.' He looked around him. 'Let's take a dander over to the stile by the next field, and I'll explain it all to you when we're sitting down.'

We settled ourselves on the stile. It was a fresh, spring day, but not specially warm, and the dew was still on the grass. 'I hope the story isn't too long, Seamus,' I said. 'Maybe we could move to my cottage for a cup of something hot, presently.'

'That's a fine idea, Jamie,' Seamus said. 'But it won't be all that long. It begins a long time ago, when I was still a young man, and not so set then on staying single as I have been since.

'It was around this time of year, and all the young lads were thinking about whether or not they should send a Valentine, and if so, who they should send it to. It wasn't so much a matter of cards, in those days. Folks still liked to send flowers or sweeties, that is, if they could afford to. Most of them ended up picking a bunch of the new spring flowers in the fields, for not only was that the cheapest way, it was the most romantic as well. Or so the youngsters round Ardnakil used to think.

There were some right pretty girls living in the village at that time, and the prettiest of all, to my mind, was young Roisin O'Flaherty. I had had my eye on her for some time. Trouble was, so had most of the rest of the young lads in the district.

It seemed to me that with Valentine's Day coming up, it was the perfect opportunity to show Roisin how I felt about her.

I intended to pick as good a bunch of flowers as I could find for her. But at the same time, I reckoned it would be a good move to go into the town, and buy the biggest and best card in the shop to give to her as well. Girls like to think you've gone to extra trouble for them.

Now, there was one lad in particular who was my chief rival for Roisin, or so I thought. This was Liam O'Reilly, a good looking fellow who rode a motor cycle and thought he was a cut above the rest of us because he worked in Murphy's garage and was training under Barney Murphy to be a mechanic. Liam was earning good money and would likely buy Roisin something expensive by way of a Valentine.

11 Two Different Valentines

Worse than that, I'd seen the way she looked at him, and only a few days ago she'd accepted a lift home from the parish supper with Liam, on that same motorbike.

But for all that, she'd agreed to go with me to the Spring Fair, and she'd given me some nice looks, as well, so I thought as between me and Liam, it was fairly evenly balanced.

It was up to me to swing the balance my way, if I could.

A couple of days before Valentine's Day I went into town. I had saved enough for a pretty fancy card, and I spent a long time picking out the best one.

I wrote on it in my best handwriting,

> *Roses are red, violets are blue,*
> *Sugar is sweet and so are you.*

Then I sealed the envelope, wrote S.W.A.L.K. on it (Sealed With a Loving Kiss), and put it away safely, ready to deliver on the day.

On February the fourteenth, I got up really early, so as to get my choice of the best blossoms in the fields, and I picked a bunch that I was certain no one would beat.

I took them home with me and struck them in water while I got myself well dressed up.

I was just putting the finishing touches to my fancy tie when I heard someone crying, not far from my open back window.

Not everyone would have heard it, maybe.

But I have pretty sharp ears, and I was in no doubt about what I was hearing.

I went out and round to the back of my cottage, and I still had the bunch of flowers in my hand.

It took me a minute or two to identify the figure lying full length, face down, on the grass by my garden hedge, crying as if her heart would break.

It was young Mary Doherty.

Now, Mary was a nice lass if ever there was one.

But I have to admit that Mary, at this stage in her life, was what you would have to call a plain, unattractive girl. She was a bit fat – well, more than a bit – and she seemed always to be covered in spots.

And right at this moment, what with her round face, and the spots on her cheeks and the end of her chin, to say nothing of the red eyes

The Seanachie: Tales of Old Seamus – *Gerry McCullough*

and nose that all this crying was giving her, I should think she'd never looked worse.

'Mary, Mary!' I said, sitting down beside her. 'Whatever's the trouble? Is someone sick? Or what is it?'

'Ah, no, Seamus!' she answered me, sitting up straight and rubbing at her eyes and her nose, making matters worse, really. 'You'll think I'm awful selfish. I should be thankful that it's nothing as bad as that.'

'Well, tell me what it is, then, Mary,' I said.

'You won't laugh, Seamus?'

'No, I won't laugh, Mary.' I had a bit of an idea, now, what was coming.

'It's Valentine's Day, Seamus, and all the girls will be getting Valentines – except me! No one ever gives me a Valentine. They think I'm too ugly!'

She burst out crying again.

I put my arm round her, and patted her shoulder. 'Nonsense, Mary,' I said, 'nobody thinks you're ugly. You're young yet. In a year or too, you'll have stopped getting spots, and the puppy fat will drop off you, and you wait and see what a pretty girl you'll be then. You'll have all the boys after you, and you'll be able to pick and choose. And what's more,' I said, 'you needn't think no one is going to give you a Valentine this year, because, look, I have something for you right here.'

And I brought the bunch of flowers forward under her nose and pushed them into her hands.

Well, if I'd wanted a reward, I got it straight away, when I saw the beaming face she turned up to me.

'Ah, thank you, Seamus,' she half whispered. The wide smile she gave me made her look right pretty already.

Then she scrambled up, and took to her heels away home to show everyone her Valentine present.

Now, time was going on, and although I didn't for one minute regret giving young Mary the flowers, still, it had left me in a bit of a fix. I went out into the fields again, looking for more, but others had been before me by now.

Search as I might, I couldn't get a decent bunch together, and it was a question whether I should give Roisin the small posy of not very fresh flowers I had managed to collect, or whether I should leave the flowers at home and rely on my extra special card.

11 Two Different Valentines

In the end, knowing Roisin could be a bit picky about the things people gave her, being used to the best, I stuck the flowers in water and left them in my cottage.

Then I gathered up the card in its envelope and went calling.

I was later than I'd meant to be, and I was annoyed to see Liam O'Reilly's motor bike parked outside the O'Flaherty's house when I got there.

However, it couldn't be helped, and I was confident that my card would do the trick, being far better than anything Liam O'Reilly would have brought Roisin.

Mrs. O'Flaherty opened the door.

'Another one for Roisin, is it?' she said. 'There's been nothing but rapping at the door all day. Come on in, Seamus, she's in the front parlour.'

Roisin was sitting in the parlour, to be sure, but so was what seemed to be half the young fellows in the neighbourhood.

I licked my lips a bit nervously, but I could see, looking round, that none of the cards on display were anything like as big or as fancy as the one I was carrying.

So I got up a bit of confidence, and when Roisin stood up and came forward to say hello to me, I produced the card from behind my back with a flourish.

'What, no flowers, Seamus?' she asked me, with a bit of a pout.

'Just you open the card, Roisin,' I said to her, doing my best to look more confident than ever. 'With a card like this one, there's no need for flowers as well. This card will tell you all you need to know about what I think of you.'

Roisin smiled. She took the card in her hands, and began to open it.

All eyes were on her, and I was glad to see that Liam O'Reilly looked a bit let down when he saw the size of the card as Roisin slid it out of the envelope.

Roisin opened the card and began to read it.

For a moment I couldn't remember what it said.

Then it came back to me.

> *Roses are red, violets are blue,*
> *Sugar is sweet and so are you.*

The Seanachie: Tales of Old Seamus – *Gerry McCullough*

There had been something else, printed inside by the shop, but I hadn't bothered to read that. I had just picked the biggest card there, and the one with the prettiest picture – a girl with dark hair like Roisin and a smiling face.

I was waiting happily for Roisin's comments, when she suddenly shrieked. She collapsed onto the sofa, put her hands to her face, and began to wail.

'How dare you, Seamus O'Hare! How dare you!'

I gaped at her, my mouth hanging open.

Then she sprang up again, and went for me like a wild beast.

Her right hand caught me a crack across the face, and as I staggered back, she began to push at me.

'Get out of this house!' she raged. 'And take your stupid card with you! I suppose you think you're very funny! Well, I don't, and I don't want to ever speak to you again! Liam's asked me to the Spring Fair, and I'm going to go with him! Go on, get out!'

I stumbled out of the house, clutching the card which she had thrust back into my hands, unable to make any sense of what had been happening.

It was only when I reached my own cottage that I pulled myself together enough to look at the card, trying to see what had upset Roisin so much.

Then I burst out laughing.

It served me right for not reading the card properly. I'd been so concerned to get the biggest one there, that I hadn't noticed that the one I'd chosen was one of those 'humorous' cards.

The picture outside was of a very pretty girl, to be sure.

Beneath it the message read,

> *'No one else looks like you!*
> *You're one in a million ...'*

But inside was a picture of a mirror, with a sort of flap covering it, and the rest of the message said,

> *'... I've attached a mirror inside*
> *to let you see for yourself!*
> *Just raise the flap!'*

Under the flap was a drawing of a very large, hairy ape.

11 Two Different Valentines

It had only taken Roisin a second to work out that I was saying she looked like an ape.

If only, I thought, I'd had the sense to look under the flap, instead of being so concentrated on what I wanted to write on it!

Or if only, even, I hadn't given the flowers to Mary. That might have made up to Roisin for the mistake, and helped her to see that I hadn't meant it.

But, no. I wasn't sorry to have given the flowers to Mary. Her beaming face came back to me, and I felt myself cheering up the more I remembered it.

And I'll tell you something, Jamie. The more I remembered Roisin's face, by contrast, when she leapt at me like a wild beast, the more I realised that maybe it was all for the best.

Supposing the card had been okay, and as a result I'd started to go out with the wildcat that she was, and ended up married to her before I found out. Pretty and all as Roisin was, the real girl underneath matched up more to the wild ape in the picture than I would ever have realised.

Maybe, after all, what had happened was the closest escape of my life!

No, I didn't marry Mary, either. She was a nice enough girl, but after my experience with Roisin, I wasn't for taking any more risks. Who knew what Mary might have been like if she'd been annoyed with me about anything? Or what she would have been like over the breakfast table?

Mary married a friend of mine, Brian Duffy, about five years later, when sure enough she'd lost her spots and her puppy fat.

Not that she was ever the equal of Roisin O'Flaherty for looks.

But I've always been grateful to her for the part she played in opening my eyes, and in my narrow escape, so every Valentine's Day, I get her a bunch of the best of the early spring flowers.

Who knows, if I hadn't got such a scare over Roisin, I might have ended up with Mary after all.

And to tell you the truth, I still have a soft spot in my heart for her.

Brian Duffy doesn't mind. He knows nothing and no one could stop me now from being a confirmed bachelor for the rest of my life. I know better than ever to risk a catastrophe like that again! You may be looking at a right pretty girl on the outside, but you never know what you'll see when you open up the card properly and look under the cover!'

12 Miss O'Sullivan's Secret

The setting sun threw its warm pink and golden rays through the window of my small cottage, as I sat one late Spring evening drinking coffee with my old friend Seamus O'Hare. We had been sitting by a turf fire, for the evenings were still chilly, discussing everything you could think of, and at last Seamus said with a laugh, 'Look, Jamie! We've

> *'... tired the sun with talking,*
> *And sent it down the sky.'*

More and more as the years went by I had come to value the times, during my irregular visits to the cottage I owned in the little Donegal town of Ardnakil, when I could sit like this with old Seamus, sharing our thoughts, and often – for Seamus was a born story teller, a Seanachie – listening to one of his tales of by-gone days.

At the thought, I said lazily to him, 'It's a while since I heard one of your stories, Seamus. Have you run out?'

Seamus laughed, and stroked the short curly grey-white beard which adorned his chin.

'Never!' he said. 'Give me a subject and just let me get started!'

I laughed in turn.

'You told me once, Seamus, that you spent most of your school-days escaping from the classroom and roaming the countryside, and yet you've just quoted some lines to me from a poet most people have never heard of! Have you a story to explain that, I wonder?'

Seamus gazed into the dying fire for a brief moment, and I saw the memories come crowding in on him. Then he looked up, and his face wore its more usual cheeky grin.

'Indeed and I have, Jamie!' he said. 'It's true I didn't like school, for most of my time there, but there was one year, no more, when I

The Seanachie: Tales of Old Seamus – *Gerry McCullough*

enjoyed it well enough, and anything I know I suppose I learnt during that year. And the reason for that was the new schoolmistress.

Her name was Mary O'Sullivan – Miss O'Sullivan to us – and that's how I still think of her. She arrived at the school on a bright day in September at the beginning of the autumn term, when I must have been about nine years old, I suppose. The school inspector brought her in and introduced her to us, and I remember that he was bubbling over with enthusiasm for her, which wasn't one bit like the man. Timothy Groat, known to us kids as old Goatface, was as sour tempered as a cat who'd lost her kittens, and as liable to scratch.

'You may think yourselves lucky to have Miss O'Sullivan to teach you this year, boys and girls,' he ended up, 'for she's got a list of qualifications a mile long, and at the end of this year she's off to Dublin to add another one to the list, a degree from the University, no less!'

Then he bowed himself out and left Miss O'Sullivan to take control, and to live up to his glowing recommendation.

And indeed she did. She was a slight, dark-haired wisp of a girl, not more than nineteen, I can realise with hindsight, but to us kids, of course, she was an adult, on the other side of the great divide from childhood. She was pretty, too. She put me in mind of the fairy princess in the big book of Fairy Tales with the coloured illustrations, that I'd sneaked out of the reward box at the back of the classroom last year, and managed to read part of while I was supposed to be learning my tables, before the teacher caught me.

And she was a great teacher.

She could keep control without using the cane, because her lessons were interesting.

She had us bringing wild flowers and things into the classroom to find out more about them, she read to us in a way that brought the characters and the plots to life, and she let us act out the roles in history lessons, a thing we had never done before.

She was interested in our opinions, too, something no other adult had ever been.

And above all, she had a smile like an angel, and she was always ready with help and sympathy when it was needed.

Ah, Miss O'Sullivan was a great girl, indeed.

I don't remember how I came to know that she was working at our little village school for a year in order to save enough money to go to

12 Miss O'Sullivan's Secret

the Teachers' Training College and get herself a proper qualification, for all old Goatface's talk about her seemed to have been dreamed up out of his own head. She had no qualifications except her own wisdom and enthusiasm. But sure, those were enough, and no one had anything to complain about in the job she was doing.

I think maybe she told me a bit about herself, one day after school, when she found me crying. I'm not ashamed to mention it after such a space of years, for I was still very young, and if a child can't be allowed to cry sometimes, then who can? She sat on the bench beside me and put her arm round me, and I shared with her my despair in ever learning anything, for, as I told her, I'd wasted too much time up till then in missing school and roaming about in a heedless manner, and how would I ever pass exams and get grand qualifications like herself? For she had fired me up with the desire to be a school teacher myself when I grew up.

She didn't laugh at me, Jamie, as I see you're doing, you rogue, but instead she said, 'Don't be saying you've wasted your time, Seamus, for young as you are I've never met anyone who knows as much about the countryside as you do.'

I can tell you she amazed me, yes, and cheered me up more than you might believe, and I think it was then that she went on to say that exams weren't everything, and to tell me that she herself had no qualifications as yet, though she hoped to get one next year. And if I was prepared to work hard, she said, there was no reason why I shouldn't start to pass exams and get whatever qualifications I wanted in the end, 'for,' she said, 'you're one of the brightest boys in the class, Seamus, and don't let anyone tell you different!'

I never told anyone what she'd said about her lack of any actual qualifications, of course. I knew without her telling me that it was a secret between her and me, and I was all the more delighted that she should have trusted me with it.

It was a good year, the only time I ever enjoyed school, as I said, for after Miss O'Sullivan left I'm afraid I went back to my wicked ways and was absent more than present. The only bad thing about the year was that it went so quickly, and before I knew it, there was only a month or so till Miss O'Sullivan would be leaving.

One afternoon I had stayed behind after class to finish a drawing I was doing for her of a swallow, when I heard someone talking to her.

The Seanachie: Tales of Old Seamus – *Gerry McCullough*

I was fairly out of sight, behind the big screen where Miss O'Sullivan pinned up the best of our drawings, when I heard old Goatface.

He was speaking in a soft, wheedling sort of voice which sounded so unlike the old rascal that I was taken by surprise. Then his voice got louder, and I could tell that he was angry about something.

'You needn't try to fool me, girl!' he was shouting. 'I know all about your tricks. I know you aren't who you claimed to be. I've got the documents to prove it! You don't have any qualifications, and if the School Board knew they'd have you thrown out of here faster than a cat can lick its tail!' Then his voice suddenly dropped again, and I could hear him say, 'Ah, Mary, my dear, where's the need for you and me to quarrel? Sure, can't we be friends, and no need for the Board ever to see these documents? How about a nice friendly kiss, now?'

Then there was a scuffling noise and then all of a sudden a ringing slap and a squawk out of old Goatface you could have heard in Donegal Town.

I was peeping cautiously out from behind the big screen by this time, and I can tell you I was nearly knocked over in the rush by old Goatface, who was getting himself up from the floor where Miss O'Sullivan seemed to have pushed him, and out of the room.

I picked myself up in turn, and there was Miss O'Sullivan sitting with her face in her hands and weeping in despair.

I went over and put my arm round her to comfort her, just as she had done to me. 'Don't cry, Miss,' was all I could think of to say, but it seemed to be enough, for presently she lifted her face and tried to smile at me, though the tears were still flowing.

'Ah, Seamus, you're a good, kind boy,' she said.

'Maybe there's something I can do to help, Miss?' I ventured to ask.

'Nobody can help, Seamus,' she sighed. 'It's all my own stupid fault. I thought I was being so clever! But it was wrong, and I've got my just deserts.'

She looked at me unhappily.

'You heard what Mr Groat was saying?'

'Some of it,' I admitted.

'You see, Seamus, I don't have any proper qualifications for this job. I told you that once, didn't I? I don't know if you ever wondered how I came to be here, in that case? I'll tell you how, Seamus. I lied about it. My cousin, another Mary, but with the surname of O'Sullivan,

12 Miss O'Sullivan's Secret

has all the qualifications I claimed to have. She emigrated to America last year, and when I came to apply for this job, I took her name and qualifications, and they were delighted to get me, as I knew they would be. All I wanted was the wages for a year, so I could pay for a course in teacher training for myself. But I've been well served. Mr Groat found out somehow or other that I'm only Mary Hagan, without a letter to my name, and no way fit for the work I've been doing.'

'Yes, you are, Miss!' I exclaimed. 'You're the best teacher we've ever had here!'

She laughed. 'It cheers me to hear you say that, Seamus. Well, maybe I've done some good then, with all my faults. Anyway, you won't have me any longer. Groat has two photographs, one of me and one of my cousin, and what's more he has a statement signed by my aunt identifying which of them is which. I'm sure she meant no harm in writing it, she wouldn't have understood why he wanted it, I know.

She'll have gone to America herself by now to join my cousin Mary. Groat must have just caught her in time. Funny to think that if he'd been a few days later looking for her, he wouldn't have got his evidence! Well, there it is. He just has to show those things to the School Board and I'll be sacked, and without the rest of the term's wages, too. So no college for me, I'm afraid.'

'Don't you worry, Miss!' I said grimly. 'I'm not going to let old Goatface get away with it!'

'Old Goatface? Is that what you call him?' Miss O'Sullivan – I still thought of her as that – giggled, and suddenly seemed like a little girl. 'He is an old goat, isn't he?'

I didn't quite know what I was going to do, but a few ideas were filtering through my brain. Young as I was, I knew that what I had overheard was an attempt by old Goatface to blackmail the schoolmistress, in a particularly unpleasant way, not looking for money, but for her to let him make love to her, and I was determined not to see it succeed.

There was no way, of course, that Miss O'Sullivan would have anything to do with the nasty old man, but I was determined that he wouldn't get to have his revenge on her, and get her kicked out of the school, and lose her chance of earning a proper qualification at the Teachers' Training College. Okay, she shouldn't have lied, but she

The Seanachie: Tales of Old Seamus – *Gerry McCullough*

realised that now herself. If we all got what we deserved, there's none of us would get off lightly. I couldn't bear to see her punished further.

Well, she gave me a quick hug, and sat up and wiped her eyes.

'Don't you worry any more about it, Seamus,' she said. 'If that's the way it's going to be, I'll just have to put up with it.'

'Not if I have anything to do with it, Miss,' I told her, but she only gave me a half-hearted grin through the rest of her tears, and said, 'You're a great boy, Seamus, but don't be worrying any more about it.'

I went home and gave the matter some thought. Then, as an idea began to stir in my head, I went out into the garden and collected a bucket of whitewash that I knew was kept in the shed. Then I went round to my friend Paddy Lenahan's and borrowed his dog Scruffy. Scruffy was a big black mongrel with a mixture of labrador and collie, a friendly, boisterous animal with, I knew, only one bad thing about him, and that was his attitude to cats, who he hated with an unworthy zeal.

Then I headed for old Goatface's cottage on the other side of the village.

Old Goatface, I knew, had a cat called Lucifer who was probably the only creature, besides himself, that he cared about.

I knocked on the door, the pail of whitewash hanging from one hand, and my other hand in Scruffy's collar, holding him back as much out of sight as I could manage until the door was properly open.

'Who's there?' came old Goatface's voice, sounding suspicious and grouchy, as usual. 'I'm busy here with some paperwork! Can't you come back later, whoever you are?'

I paid no attention, but rapped firmly on the door again.

A moment later, Goatface peered suspiciously round the half open door. In one hand, I was glad to see, he was clutching a few papers, two of which looked like signed photographs and the third a handwritten document of some sort.

'Please sir, Mr Groat sir,' I began, 'could I earn a few pennies from you by slapping a fresh coat of whitewash on the walls of your cottage, sir?'

Goatface was never one to miss a bargain.

'Why, certainly, boy!' he exclaimed, and pulled the door further open.

Scruffy, my hand released from his collar, shot through the opening.

12 Miss O'Sullivan's Secret

He could not only hear but smell Lucifer, one of his favourite enemies, and he bounded into the room enthusiastically, knocking Goatface over onto his back, and leaving him lying, both feet high in the air, just inside the front door. A gust of wind came into the cottage with Scruffy, and sent papers, a vase full of flowers, and some books that had been left open on old Goatface's desk, blowing in all directions.

Uttering cries of pretended horror, I rushed after the large, bounding animal, who was chock full of excitement and the hunter's instinct.

'Stop, stop, you heathen!' I bawled at him. 'Where did you come from? Get back out of here, before I murder you!'

Lucifer, howling, leapt for the top of the nearest cupboard.

Scruffy, fresh and excited, leapt after him, barking noisily.

Old Goatface recovered his balance, staggered to his feet, rubbing at the sore parts of his anatomy, and went after the two animals as quickly as he could, yelping louder than either of the pair of them.

I chased after them all, making sure I added as much as possible to the noise and confusion.

It was only when I had caught hold of Scruffy and the noise had died down slightly, that it became apparent that in knocking into Old Goatface, Scruffy had caused him to drop the papers he had been holding in his hand.

And in looking for somewhere to set my bucket of whitewash down out of the way, I seemed to have managed to slop most of the contents over the paper and the photographs, which were now unrecognisable.

'Oh, sir!' I exclaimed distressfully. 'Your papers! They're ruined!'

I grabbed them up from the floor.

'Here, maybe I could shake off some of the mess into the fire!'

As I spoke, I was rushing towards the fireplace, and somehow I had let go of Scruffy's collar again. Scruffy enthusiastically sprang once more after Lucifer. It happened that he knocked against my elbow. The next moment the papers in my hand had shot into the fireplace, and were instantly consumed in flames.

I apologised to old Goatface profusely, and offered to whitewash his walls for free to make up for it, but he still seemed unreasonably angry.

Clearly, as I'd managed to make sure when I glanced at them quickly as I picked them up from the cottage floor and pretended to shake the whitewash off them, the photos and papers were the evidence he'd got hold of from Miss O'Sullivan's aunt, showing that she was really Mary Hagan. The evidence that he wanted to use to blackmail my teacher, or else have his revenge on her by having her thrown out of the school.

Old Goatface was gibbering with rage, and for some reason he seemed to think it was all my fault, as if I'd ruined his evidence on purpose.

But after all, as I pointed out to him, I'd probably saved Lucifer's life by holding back the stray dog who'd broken into his cottage. And as I told him, when you're rushing about trying to prevent a stray dog, who's doing his best to murder a poor little innocent cat, you can't stop to think out just where exactly you're going to set your bucket of whitewash!

About the author

Gerry McCullough has been writing poems and stories since childhood. Brought up in north Belfast, she graduated in English and Philosophy from Queen's University, Belfast, then went on to gain an MA in English.

She lives just outside Belfast, in Northern Ireland, has four grown up children and is married to author, media producer and broadcaster, Raymond McCullough, with whom she co-edited the Irish magazine, *Bread*, (published by *Kingdom Come Trust*), from 1990-96. In 1995 they published a non-fiction book called, *Ireland – now the good news!*

Over the past few years Gerry has had more than fifty short stories published in UK, Irish and American magazines, anthologies and annuals – as well as broadcast on *BBC Radio Ulster* – plus poems and articles published in several Northern Ireland and UK magazines. She has also read from her novel, poems and short stories at several Irish literary events.

Gerry won the *Cúirt International Literary Award* for 2005 (Galway); was shortlisted for the 2008 *Brian Moore Award* (Belfast); shortlisted for the 2009 *Cúirt Award*; and commended in the 2009 *Seán O'Faolain Short Story Competition*, (Cork).

Belfast Girls, her first full-length Irish novel, was first published (by *Night Publishing*, UK) in November 2010. *Danger Danger* was published by *Precious Oil Publications* in October 2011; followed by *The Seanachie: Tales of Old Seamus* in January 2012 (a first collection of humorous Irish short stories, previously published in a weekly Irish magazine); and *Angel in Flight* (the first Angel Murphy thriller) in June 2012.

The *Cúirt Award* winning story, *Primroses*, and the *Seán O'Faolain* commended story, *Giving Up*, will be included in a new collection of twelve Irish short stories written by Gerry, to be published shortly. Also in the pipeline are, *Lady Molly and the Snapper* – a young adult novel set in Dublin; and *Not the End of the World* – a humorous, futuristic, adult fantasy novel.

More info at: ***gerrymccullough.com   gerrysbooks.blogspot.com***

Belfast Girls

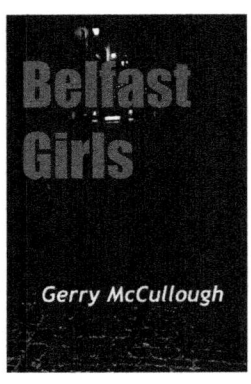

The story of three girls – Sheila, Phil and Mary – growing up into the new emerging post-conflict Belfast of money, drugs, high fashion and crime; and of their lives and loves.

Sheila, a supermodel, is kidnapped. Phil is sent to prison. Mary, surviving a drug overdose, has a spiritual awakening.

It is also the story of the men who matter to them –

John Branagh, former candidate for the priesthood, a modern Darcy, someone to love or hate. Will he and Sheila ever get together? Davy Hagan, drug dealer, 'mad, bad and dangerous to know'. Is Phil also mad to have anything to do with him?

Although from different religious backgrounds, starting off as childhood friends, the girls manage to hold on to that friendship in spite of everything.

A book about contemporary Ireland and modern life. A book which both men and women can enjoy – thriller, romance, comedy, drama – and much more ….

"fascinating ... original ... multilayered ... expertly travels from one genre to the next"
Kellie Chambers, Ulster Tatler *(Book of the Month)*

"romance at the core ... enriched with breathtaking action, mystery, suspense and some tear-jerking moments of tragedy.
Sheila M. Belshaw, *author*

"What starts out as a crime thriller quickly evolves into a literary festival beyond the boundary of genres"
PD Allen, *author*

Belfast Girls

Gerry McCullough

Chapter 1

Jan 21, 2007

The street lights of Belfast glistened on the dark pavements where, even now, with the troubles officially over, few people cared to walk alone at night. John Branagh drove slowly, care-fully, through the icy streets.

In the distance, he could see the lights of the Magnifico Hotel, a bright contrasting centre of noise, warmth and colour.

He felt again the excitement of the news he'd heard today.

Hey, he'd actually made the grade at last – full-time reporter for BBC TV, right there on the local news programme, not just a trainee, any longer. Unbelievable.

The back end shifted a little as he turned a corner. He gripped the wheel tighter and slowed down even more. There was black ice on the roads tonight. Gotta be careful.

So, he needed to work hard, show them he was keen. This interview, now, in this hotel? This guy Speers? If it turned out good enough, maybe he could go back to Fat Barney and twist his arm, get him to commission it for local TV, the Hearts and Minds programme maybe? Or even – he let his ambition soar – go national? Or how's about one of those specials everybody seemed to be into right now?

There were other thoughts in his mind but as usual he pushed them down out of sight. Sheila Doherty would be somewhere in the hotel tonight, but he had plenty of other stuff to think about to steer his attention away from past unhappiness. No need to focus on anything right now but his career and its hopeful prospects.

Montgomery Speers, better get the name right, new Member of the Legislative Assembly, wanted to give his personal views on the peace process and how it was working out. Yeah. Wanted some publicity, more like. Anti, of course, or who'd care? But that was just how people were.

John curled his lip. He had to follow it up. It could give his career the kick start it needed.

But he didn't have to like it.

* * *

Inside the Magnifico Hotel, in the centre of newly regenerated Belfast, all was bustle and chatter, especially in the crowded space behind the catwalk. The familiar fashion show smell, a mixture of cosmetics and hair dryers, was overwhelming.

Sheila Doherty sat before her mirror, and felt a cold wave of unhappiness surge over her. How ironic it was, that title the papers gave her, today's most super supermodel. She closed her eyes and put her hands to her ears, trying to shut everything out for just one snatched moment of peace and silence.

Every now and then it came again. The pain. The despair. A face hovered before her mind's eye, the white, angry face of John Branagh, dark hair falling forward over his furious grey eyes. She deliberately blocked the thought, opening her eyes again. She needed to slip on the mask, get ready to continue on the surface of things where her life was perfect.

"Comb that curl over more to the side, will you, Chrissie?" she asked, "so it shows in front of my ear. Yeah, that's right – if you just spray it there – thanks, pet."

The hairdresser obediently fixed the curl in place. Sheila's long red-gold hair gleamed in the reflection of three mirrors positioned to show every angle. Everything had to be perfect – as perfect as her life was supposed to be. The occasion was too important to allow for mistakes.

Her fine-boned face with its clear translucent skin, like ivory, and crowned with the startling contrast of her hair, looked back at her from the mirror, green eyes shining between thick black lashes – black only because of the mascara.

She examined herself critically, considering her appearance as if it were an artefact which had to be without flaw to pass a test.

She stood up. "Brilliant, pet," she said. "Now the dress." The woman held out the dress for Sheila to step into, then carefully

Chapter 1

pulled the ivory satin shape up around the slim body and zipped it at the back. The dress flowed round her, taking and emphasising her long fluid lines, her body slight and fragile as a daydream. She walked over to the door, ready to emerge onto the catwalk. She was very aware that this was the most important moment of one of the major fashion shows of her year.

The lights in the body of the hall were dimmed, those focussed on the catwalk went up, and music cut loudly through the sudden silence. Francis Delmara stepped forward and began to introduce his new spring line.

For Sheila, ready now for some minutes and waiting just out of sight, the tension revealed itself as a creeping feeling along her spine. She felt suddenly cold and her stomach fluttered.

It was time and, dead on cue, she stepped lightly out onto the catwalk and stood holding the pose for a long five seconds, as instructed, before swirling forward to allow possible buyers a fuller view.

She was greeted by gasps of admiration, then a burst of applause. Ignoring the reaction, she kept her head held high, her face calm and remote, as far above human passion as some elusive, intangible figure of Celtic myth, a Sidhe, a dweller in the hollow hills, distant beyond man's possessing – just as Delmara had taught her. This was her own individual style, the style which had earned her the nickname 'Ice Maiden' from the American journalist Harrington Smith. She moved forward along the catwalk, turned this way and that, and finally swept a low curtsey to the audience before standing there, poised and motionless.

Delmara was silent at first to allow the sight of Sheila in one of his most beautiful creations its maximum impact. Then he began to draw attention to the various details of the dress.

It was time for Sheila to withdraw. Once out of sight, she began a swift, organised change to her next outfit, while Delmara's other models were in front.

No time yet for her to relax, but the show seemed set for success.

* * *

MLA, Montgomery Speers, sitting in the first row of seats, the celebrity seats, with his latest blonde girlfriend by his side, allowed himself to feel relieved.

Francis Delmara had persuaded him to put money into Delmara Fashions and particularly into financing Delmara's supermodel, Sheila Doherty, and he was present tonight in order to see for himself if his investment was safe. He thought, even so early in the show, that it was.

He was a broad shouldered man in his early forties, medium height, medium build, red-cheeked, and running slightly to fat. There was nothing particularly striking about his appearance except for the piercing dark eyes set beneath heavy, jutting eyebrows. His impressive presence stemmed from his personality, from the aura of power and aggression which surrounded him.

A businessman first and foremost, he had flirted with political involvement for several years. He had stood successfully for election to the local council, feeling the water cautiously with one toe while he made up his mind. Would he take the plunge and throw himself whole-heartedly into politics?

The new Assembly gave him his opportunity, if he wanted to take it. More than one of the constituencies offered him the chance to stand for a seat. He was a financial power in several different towns where his computer hardware companies provided much needed jobs. He was elected to the seat of his choice with no trouble. The next move was to build up his profile, grab an important post once things got going, and progress up the hierarchy.

In an hour or so, when the Fashion Show was over, he would meet this young TV reporter for some preliminary discussion of a possible interview or of an appearance on a discussion panel. He was slightly annoyed that someone so junior had been lined up to talk to him. John Branagh, that was the name, wasn't it? Never heard of him. Should have been someone better known, at least. Still, this was only the preliminary. They would roll out the big guns for him soon enough when he was more firmly established. Meanwhile his thoughts lingered on the beautiful Sheila Doherty.

If he wanted her, he could buy her, he was sure. And more and more as he watched her, he knew that, yes, he wanted her.

* * *

Chapter 1

A fifteen minute break, while the audience drank the free wine and ate the free canapés. Behind the scenes again, Sheila checked hair and makeup. A small mascara smear needed to be removed, a touch more blusher applied. In a few minutes she was ready but something held her back.

She stared at herself in the mirror and saw a cool, beautiful woman, the epitome of poise and grace. She knew that famous, rich, important men over two continents would give all their wealth and status to possess her, or so they said. She was an icon according to the papers. That meant, surely, something unreal, something artificial, painted or made of stone.

And what was the good? There was only one man she wanted. John Branagh. And he'd pushed her away. He believed she was a whore – a tart – someone not worth touching. What did she do to deserve that?

It wasn't fair! she told herself passionately. He went by rules that were medieval. No-one nowadays thought the odd kiss mattered that much. Oh, she was wrong. She'd hurt him, she knew she had. But if he'd given her half a chance, she'd have apologised – told him how sorry she was. Instead of that, he'd called her such names – how could she still love him after that? But she knew she did.

How did she get to this place, she wondered, the dream of romantic fiction, the dream of so many girls, a place she hated now, where men thought of her more and more as a thing, an object to be desired, not a person? When did her life go so badly wrong? She thought back to her childhood, to the skinny, ginger-haired girl she once was. Okay, she hated how she looked but otherwise, surely, she was happy. Or was that only a false memory?

"Sheila - where are you?"

The hairdresser poked her head round the door and saw Sheila with every sign of relief.

"Thank goodness! Come on, love, only got a couple of minutes! Delmara says I've to check your hair. Wants it tied back for this one."

* * *

The evening was almost at its climax. The show began with evening dress, and now it was to end with evening dress – but this time with Delmara's most beautiful and exotic lines. Sheila stood up and shook out her frock, a cloud of short ice-blue chiffon, sewn with glittering silver beads and feathers. She and Chrissie between them swept up her hair, allowing a few loose curls to hang down her back and one side of her face, fixed it swiftly into place with two combs, and clipped on more silver feathers. She fastened on long white earrings with a pearly sheen and slipped her feet into the stiletto heeled silver shoes left ready and waiting. She moved over to the doorway for her cue. There was no time to think or to feel the usual butterflies. Chloe came off and she counted to three and went on.

There was an immediate burst of applause.

To the loud music of Snow Patrol, Sheila half floated, half danced along the catwalk, her arms raised ballerina fashion. When she had given sufficient time to allow the audience their fill of gasps and appreciation, she moved back and April and Chloe appeared in frocks with a similar effect of chiffon and feathers, but with differences in style and colour. It was Delmara's spring look for evening wear and she could tell at once that the audience loved it.

The three girls danced and circled each other, striking dramatic poses as the music died down sufficiently to allow Delmara to comment on the different features of the frocks.

With one part of her mind Sheila was aware of the audience, warm and relaxed now, full of good food and drink, their minds absorbed in beauty and fashion, ready to spend a lot of money. Dimly in the background she heard the sounds of voices shouting and feet running.

The door to the ballroom burst open. People began to scream. It was something Sheila had heard about for years now, the

subject of local black humour, but had never before seen. Three figures, black tights pulled over flattened faces as masks, uniformly terrifying in black leather jackets and jeans, surged into the

room. The three sub-machine guns cradled in their arms sent deafening

bursts of gunfire upwards. Falling plaster dust and stifling clouds of gun smoke filled the air.

For one long second they stood just inside the entrance way, crouched over their weapons, looking round. One of them stepped forward and grabbed Montgomery Speers by the arm.

Chapter 1

"Move it, mister!" he said. He dragged Speers forcefully to one side, the weapon poking him hard in the chest.

A second man gestured roughly with his gun in the general direction of Sheila.

"You!" he said harshly. "Yes, you with the red hair! Get over here!

###

Buy **Belfast Girls** now on *Amazon*

(paperback and *Kindle* editions)

Danger Danger

Two lives in parallel – twin sisters separated at birth, but their lives take strangely similar and dangerous roads until the final collision which hurls each of them to the edge of disaster.

Katie and her gambling boyfriend Dec find themselves threatened with peril from the people Dec has cheated.

Jo-Anne (Annie), through her boyfriend Steven, finds herself in the hands of much more dangerous crooks.

Can they survive and achieve safety and happiness?

"starts with a bang and never quite lets up on the tension ... it will hook you from the beginning and keep you spell bound until the very last sentence."
Ellen Fritz, Books 4 Tomorrow

"The emotional intensity of the characters is beautifully drawn ... You care for these people."
Stacey Danson, *author, Australia*

an amazing, page turning, stunning novel ... equal to Belfast Girls in every respect. I can't wait for her next novel to be published.
Teresa Geering, *author, UK*

an attention-grabbing plot, strong writing, and vivid characterization, ... fast-paced and highly addictive
L. Anne Carrington, *author, US*

Danger Danger

Gerry McCullough

Chapter One

Time – 14 May 88, twenty-three years ago.
Place – St. Austin's Maternity Hospital.

Marie Sinclair, aged seventeen and single, lay in a hospital bed, struggling through the first stages of childbirth.

She had been to the ante natal clinic, had learnt how to relax, had learnt all about the second stage, about panting like a dog and not pushing until the doctor or the midwife told her to push.

She had hoped that Jamie would be with her when all this was happening. She had to admit that she was scared.

Natural childbirth, that was the thing to go for, everyone had said. But right now, there were only two things she wanted. One was a hefty dose of some helpful drug, something, anything, to take away the pain.

The other was Jamie.

If he had been here to hold her hand and tell her he loved her, it would have been so much better. But he had chickened out. He'd been horrified when he found that she was pregnant. Had never suggested marrying her, even moving in with her. Didn't want a baby. And when the scan showed that there were actually two babies, he was even more reluctant.

Marie groaned loudly again. The pains were coming more strongly than ever.

The doctor offered an injection of pethedine. Marie gratefully agreed.

Everything was further away now. She could still feel the pain of the strong contractions. But it felt as if they were happening to someone else. Someone miles away. Then suddenly she could hear the midwife calling out to her loudly.

Danger Danger – Gerry McCullough

'Marie! Marie!'

She listened with an effort.

'Don't push! Don't push!'

It was almost impossible to obey. The urge to push was almost overwhelming.

Marie remembered her ante-natal training. Pant like a dog.

She panted. Panted some more. Went on panting.

Then, 'Good girl!' It was the midwife, speaking from so far away. 'One more effort, now. Push!'

The second baby came flying out, fielded dextrously by the midwife. Then the afterbirth.

And then peace, and a time of rest.

Marie slept.

When she at last surfaced, there were two tiny babies in two cots, one on either side of her bed.

Marie gazed at them in awe. How beautiful they were. But how could she look after two?

She remembered that she had arranged that one of the babies should be adopted. She couldn't bear to think of giving up both. Now, with a pang, she realised that she didn't want to give up either.

Her mum had offered to help, so that Marie could go back to school, get qualifications for a decent job in the future. But only if Marie didn't keep both babies. Mum could only help if Marie only kept one. Mum had made it clear that two babies were a bit much for her to look after.

Jamie didn't want to get involved.

Marie was frightened. She had been set against abortion. It was murder, nothing else. But here she was with two beautiful babies, and a decision to make. She didn't even know if they were boys or girls.

If they were one of each, she would keep the girl, she thought suddenly. It seemed, somehow, as if that would be easier.

A nurse peered round the bed curtains, and pulled them back enough to be able to come in.

'Awake, now?' she asked pleasantly. 'Have you held your babies yet?'

Chapter One

'No,' said Marie weakly. 'I'd like to.'

The nurse came round to Marie's left side, scooped a tiny bundle out of the cot, and placed her carefully in Marie's arms.

'A little girl,' she said, flicking back the blanket which was wrapped around the baby, to demonstrate. 'Isn't she beautiful?'

Marie gazed at her daughter. 'She's so tiny.'

An overwhelming love for the baby swept through her.

'I'll keep this one, nurse.'

The nurse looked surprised at the suddenness of the decision. But it wasn't a good idea for her to rock the boat, so she said nothing.

'I decided I'd keep the girl,' Marie said. She knew she didn't need to explain, but somehow she wanted to justify herself.

'Right,' said the nurse briskly. 'So this other one is for adoption. You have six weeks to change your mind, you know.'

'No!' said Marie. 'No! I can't keep them both. Please take the other one away now, nurse! I'll sign the forms when the six weeks are up, but I couldn't bear to have him here all that time, and get to love him. Please!'

The nurse felt that she understood. It would be better if the baby was looked after away from the new mother until the adoptive parents could legally take it. Silently she wheeled the cot out from the cubicle.

Marie continued to hold her little daughter. She would call her Catherine. Katie for short.

She felt that she had made the right decision. A girl was more helpless. A girl needed her mother.

No one had told her that the other baby was a little girl, too.

Chapter Two

Time – April 2011

Philip Bernstein stood foursquare in the centre of his den, his own personal room, in his chalet in the remote Alps of Switzerland. He was a multi-millionaire known mainly for his generous philanthropy. The chalet was many times the size of the normal Swiss home. Outside it was clean and bright, with the white walls, green folded back shutters always freshly painted, and window boxes bright with whatever flowers were in season. Inside it was warm, inviting, and furnished to the extreme of luxury. It was clear that for Philip Bernstein, philanthropy began at home.

Bernstein – he normally insisted on his title 'Mr Bernstein' to all but a few close equals – was a chubby man under average height but with an underlying steel which his friendly smiling public face often prevented people from recognising, sometimes until too late.

As well as a philanthropist he was a collector of Fine Art. A very private room in his chalet, never unlocked except by Bernstein himself, and seldom revealed to anyone else, held an amazing collection of Old Masters, Impressionists, and some of the moderns whose work he was proud to have recognised while their talent was still at the chrysalis stage.

As he stood squarely in the centre of the valuable Turkish carpet which he walked over daily, he cast impatient glances at his watch every now and then. He was being kept waiting. Only by a few minutes so far, but it was something he was not accustomed to.

He looked up as the door opened and a man came in.

'Ah, Carmichael,' he grunted.

The man who entered was slim and wiry, with reddish hair. Not small, but no more than average height. The bones of his lean face showed an underlying

Danger Danger – Gerry McCullough

strength, and the sleeves of his trim business suit hinted at the well-developed muscular force hidden beneath them.

'You wanted to speak to me, Mr Bernstein?' He spoke politely, but with no trace of apology or worry in his tone. The Irish accent came across pleasantly.

'Yes.' Mr Bernstein went over to the huge oak desk on the other side of the room and sat behind it, waving his hand at the chair in front as an indication that Carmichael should sit there. 'How long have you been working for me now, Carmichael? About six months, isn't it?'

'Six and a half.'

'You've been doing a good job.' The praise was given grudgingly, but seemed to be genuine. 'I've been thinking of moving you up – giving you a bit more responsibility. How would that suit you?'

'I'd like that.' Rory Carmichael spoke easily, showing little sign that this was what he had been eagerly working towards for that six and a half months.

'Very well. I'm sending you over to Ireland. You'll know your way around there, of course. I'm not happy with the way things have been going there. That man, McCann, who's been running the business – either he's more of a fool than I took him for, or he's been cheating me. I'll put you in overall charge. Contact McCann – not too publicly at first.

He has a boat, maybe you could hire one and arrange a rendezvous that way. Find out what he's up to. I won't be cheated. I'll let him know you're there to take over. Just don't make a mess of it, or try to cheat me yourself, Carmichael. When I deal with that sort of thing, once I'm sure about it, believe me, there are no holds barred.'

An ugly look which Carmichael had seen on Philip Bernstein's face once or twice before changed him in a second from a cuddly, cheerful Santa Claus figure into a hard, frightening man whose criminal leanings were usually carefully hidden.

'Okay, Carmichael. Make your arrangements and get off as soon as you can. Whelman will give you whatever details you need about contacting McCann.' Whelman was Mr Bernstein's valued private secretary.

The meeting was clearly over. Carmichael got up to go. As he left, he heard Bernstein speaking into the intercom on his desk. 'Send Flynn in now. I want to see him straightaway.'

###

Chapter Two

Buy **Danger Danger** now on *Amazon*
(paperback and *Kindle* editions)

Non-fiction books from

A Wee Taste a' Craic:

*All the Irish craic from the popular **Celtic Roots Radio** shows, 2-25*

Raymond McCullough

"I absolutely loved this! I found it to be very informative about Irish life culture, language and traditions."
Elinor Carlisle (author, Reading, UK)

"a unique insight into the Northern Irish people & their self deprecating sense of humour"
Strawberry, Northern Ireland

"I loved your commentary and explanations of N. Ireland's unmistakable wit and sense of humor.
Jerry McLean (Los Angeles, USA)

"My history is Irish so I love learning new things about the country!"
Sage Burnish (Athens, Georgia, USA)

The Whore and her Mother:
9/11, Babylon and the Return of the King

Raymond McCullough

Could the writings of the ancient Hebrew prophets be relevant to events taking place in the world today?

These Hebrew prophets – Isaiah, Jeremiah, Habbakuk and the apostle John, in *The Revelation* – wrote extensively about a latter day city and empire which would dominate, exploit and corrupt all the nations of the world. They referred to it as Babylon the Great, or Mega-Babylon, and they foretold that its fall – 'in one day' – would devastate the economies of the whole world. Have these prophecies been fulfilled already?

Is Mega-Babylon the Roman Catholic Church?
A world super-church?
Rebuilt ancient Babylon?
Brussels, Jerusalem, or somewhere entirely different?
Should this city/nation have a large Jewish population?
Why all the talk about merchants, cargoes, commodities, trade?

Can we rely on the words of these ancient prophets?
If so, what else did they foretell that is still to be fulfilled?
Do they refer to other major nations – USA, Russia, China, Europe?
What about militant Islam?

"AMAZED when I read this book ... in awe of your extensive knowledge on so many levels: Christian, Jewish, and Muslim culture; the Jewish diaspora ... Greek & Hebrew; ... thought-provoking and troublesome ... many will be offended, but you consistently build your case instead of being sensationalistic."
James Revoir (UK, author of *Priceless Stones*)

"Most surprisingly, I left this book with a new feeling, one of renewed hope and reassurance amidst a story of terrible tragedy. Great work!"
Shamrock "SK" (Weimar, Germany)

Ireland – now the __good__ news!

The best of *'Bread'* Vols. 1 & 2 –
personal testimonies and church/fellowship profiles from around Ireland

Edited by: *Raymond & Gerry McCullough*

"... fresh Bread – deals with the real issues facing the church in Ireland today"

Printed in Great Britain
by Amazon

40387795R00066